UNUSUAL COMPANY

UNUSUAL COMPANY

MARGARET ERHART

E. P. DUTTON NEW YORK

PUBLISHER'S NOTE: This novel is a work of fiction.
Names, characters, places, and incidents either are the
product of the author's imagination or are used fictitiously,
and any resemblance to actual persons, living or dead,
events, or locales is entirely coincidental.

Published in the United States by E. P. Dutton,
a division of NAL Penguin Inc.,
2 Park Avenue, New York, N.Y. 10016

Published simultaneously in Canada by
Fitzhenry and Whiteside, Limited, Toronto.

Library of Congress Cataloging-in-Publication Data
Erhart, Margaret.
Unusual company.
I. Title.
PS3555.R426U5   1987   813'.54   87-13423
ISBN: 0-525-24567-7

COBE

Designed by Nancy Etheredge

1 3 5 7 9 10 8 6 4 2

First Edition

Chapter 9 was previously published in Common Lives/Lesbian Lives,
Issue 22, Spring 1987; Chapter 7 was previously published in Yellow Silk:
Journal of Erotic Arts, *Issue 24, Autumn 1987.*

for Mary Clark

ACKNOWLEDGMENTS

Thanks to Bonnie Friedman and Tracy Moore, who have always been generous and loving readers; to Tony Hoagland and Charlie Smith, friends and inspiration; to Karen Heeney, who researched food and fish with inhuman patience; to Susan Lawrence, who provided unusual company; and to my unflinching parents. If not for the energy and eloquent dinners of Rita Speicher and Olga Broumas, this project never would have left home.

——

The world I wake from will never satisfy the world I wake to.

—FG

ONE

1

laire's first words to me I'll never forget. We were two strangers standing in Rizzoli's bookstore with our coats flung open, their shoulders touching as if they were already intimates, and she had a copy of *The Velveteen Rabbit* open in her hands. I was off course, searching for Botticelli in the kids' section, and when I stopped beside her she must have seen the name of the book I'd written on my palm.

"You're a long way from the Renaissance."

I had no idea she was talking to me. On the page in front of her I recognized the stuffed rabbit and the Skin Horse of the nursery tale.

"Do you know what I'd like?" she asked.

"Excuse me?"

"I'd like to trade places with a wise animal."

I had looked at her then for the first time. This was the last week of the year, and finally cold, and she was as bundled as I was. I hadn't a clue what lay beneath her huge parka and baggy pants, but I had her face, an ordinary face, not a great beauty, but with a wideness and shine about the eyes. She was a good deal taller than I. I stood to her shoulder. Her hair was long and thin, paper-bag brown as she called it. As we talked, there in the bookstore and later over coffee and tea in a nearby Hamburger Heaven, her hair kept falling in front of her shoulders and with annoyance she kept flipping it back.

That there wasn't an ounce of hesitation in her impressed me at twenty-two. I guessed she was a few years older. I saw it in the way she walked, quickly, but planting each foot with purpose, and the easy way she took my arm, this stranger, and led me through the halls of books to the front of the store. She offered me what seemed like the most unusual company I'd kept for months. She knew where we could find the world's finest devil's food cake, and sit in peace and relative quiet and become friends. Those were her words, and they, too, seemed unusual to me. I left Botticelli for another day and followed her out into the end of the afternoon in New York City.

The street made us shy, or it made Claire silent, which made me shy. We walked most of a block before she said, "This is what it's like to be thirty."

"What is what it's like? Who's thirty?"

"I am. It's like knowing too well where I'm walking, and only beginning to know who I'm walking with."

Too well, to Claire, meant being able to call up the exact bitterness of the chocolate shaved onto the sweet, devil's food frosting. In the coffee shop she smoked a few cigarettes while I ate cake. She asked me things like, "You're at least two people, aren't you? Sure you are," and "Do you think you can believe in luck and God at the same time?" The practical details of my life seemed to interest her not at all, and I never thought to ask her what she did or where she came from. Where most people would have asked about family, she wondered if I had any scars. She had a scar, she told me, though she didn't offer to show it to me, where the fateful juncture of speed, gravel and Honda had nearly killed her years ago.

She didn't have any money so I paid for the tea and coffee and cake. "If I carry money with me when I go shopping," she said, "I just end up bringing home things I don't need." She gave me a big bear hug out on the street, then caught my wrist, and I was confused for a moment and struggled to pull away until I saw how it amused her. She upturned my palm where I'd jotted that note to myself about Botticelli. "Isn't this where I leave a message?"

She wrote her address and phone number and folded my hand closed. "The phone number won't do you any good," she warned me, but I didn't give it much thought. I've never forgotten that she was the first to go that time, though I was the one with the train to catch. As long as I could see her, I watched her. I watched her hair fly back and her coat flap open. Even then, she was like a ghost in flight.

For a couple of days after I met her, I refused to believe in our encounter. As soon as it came into my mind, I put it out again. But on the third day, when I looked and saw the faint tattoo still on my palm, the numbers that resisted soap and scrubbing, I couldn't ignore her any longer, and after one attempt to call her I traveled into the city to search her out. This wasn't easy. What I finally guessed to be her apartment building was a numberless, seemingly doorless creature, slightly set back from the recently renovated buildings that lined Thompson Street; possibly held up by them as well. It rose up four stories, reminding me of the oldest boulder in the forest, crawled upon, disguised and nearly obliterated by new undergrowth.

The entrance was around the block at the back. There were the usual buttons to push to alert the occupants, but apparently the system wasn't working and the inside door was propped open with a dog-eared copy of *Reader's Digest*. I walked into a dingy front hall where a woman in a bathrobe and noisy slippers was rapidly disappearing into one of the ground-floor apartments. The door slammed. I heard several high-pitched voices laughing.

Claire had given me her apartment number, but like her telephone number, it did me no good that day. None of the doors were marked. I asked directions from one descending gentleman in a blue suit with gleaming black hair. He snorted and volunteered something in what might have been one of the Slavic languages and went on his way, holding the side of his jaw as if our exchange had caused him a sudden toothache. He smelled sweet from whatever it was he'd layered on his hair, and I followed that sweetness up to the fourth floor, where he must have lived or been visiting.

There were two doors on the fourth floor, one black like all the others in that building, and one red. Whoever she was, I decided, she would never live behind a red door, and I went back down to the third floor. No one was home in either of those apartments. I went to the second, and again finding no one, I finally went down to the first. The landlord lived in the front apartment. The sign on the door was written out in a childish script on lined yellow paper. It read:

> Do NOT ask to borrow: an egg,
> a pot or pan, a toilet plunger,
> a meat sandwich. Definitely NO MONEY!!
> Your Landlord.

I could hear soft radio music from inside, but no one came to the door. I said to it, to the scarred black paint, "I don't want to borrow anything, you old Scrooge," and turned down the hallway. But the bathrobed woman and her shrieking friends had gone out or gone to sleep. There was nothing to do but give up, and if there was a next time, hope for some sign.

This was a Sunday. Claire and I had drunk our tea and coffee together the previous Thursday. I knew the days. Time had become very precise for me, as it never had been before in my life. Which is exactly why I sought her out, my friend, my strange new acquaintance. She seemed the only thing real and solid—though infinitely mysterious!—to step between me and the rest of my twenties, which seemed like the rest of my life. I worked in my father's pet shop. I was an only child and still lived at home. I was bored by everything I knew and everyone I met, until Claire. And *she* had met *me*. I didn't let myself forget that. In the holiday free-for-all of Rizzoli's, she had singled me out.

So I tried again the next day, and only for a moment, at the sight of that same *Reader's Digest*, doubted everything, all my intentions, my expectations, every bit of my courage. It seemed foolish and careless of me not to have given her my address and telephone number as well. Would she have hopped a train to New Jersey that weekend to come see me? I wondered. And the answer that rang in the back of my head was, No.

But as soon as I was inside, events and objects began to arrange themselves in an irreversible order so that I was led on, led upstairs, led right to the red door that couldn't have been Claire's. First, a woman of almost immeasurable groceries shooed me through the tight hallway and up to the first landing simply because, with all her bundles, the only way to move out of her way was to go with her. She reminded me of some frightening piece of farm equipment that you might lose a limb to, or even your life. One good thing that came of her was that she seemed to think Claire's apartment, number 220, was on the floor above us, or on the floor above that. "Keep going," was all she said, the words seeping out of her in a little wheeze as she set the

7

first load of groceries down. She pointed emphatically at the ceiling.

I noticed something that I hadn't noticed the day before, possibly because that had been an overcast late afternoon, and this was a brighter one. I noticed that the staircase ended in a column of sunlight, or actually wound around it. The sunlight came down through a fourth-floor skylight and at this time of day turned the bannister white.

This was my second sign, and I followed it to its end like the white line of a highway. When it took me by the red door again, I stopped so suddenly I thought it possible an actual hand had reached out of that room and grabbed me. But it was only the noises. They were noises any two human beings might have made, I assured myself, and tried to move on, but the part of me that already knew Claire, knew. I stood listening for ten or fifteen minutes until the shaft of sunlight dimmed and disappeared, then I went home.

The only lovemaking I'd ever heard had been my parents', muffled by the walls between us and by the blankets I always pulled up around my ears to block it out. But this, from behind the red door, had drawn me in like a chant or hymn. I hadn't wanted to run. After the first flush of embarrassment, I had stepped closer. I had imagined what I had never dared imagine in the case of my parents, and I surprised myself with what I already knew. I was also surprised to feel the first unpleasant ache of jealousy, a burning between heart and stomach. But it kept me there as much as my curiosity did, a thief at the door weekday afternoons.

The noises began as a hum in which both voices were one, then branched out into their individual parts as they got louder. Each part moaned, an eerie, underwater moan. Each screamed, like the screaming of birds. The voices were always faint, and I could never be sure how much of what I heard was my own invention. At first I'd been afraid I'd be caught eavesdropping by the man in the blue suit, or some other neighbor, and this watchfulness ruined my concentration. But as the days went on, I relaxed. If there was traffic in the apartment building it all seemed to take place on the three floors below me. Soon the length of my visits increased—fifteen minutes, twenty, half an hour, and my ear prickled from its awkward position against the rough wood of the door. Always the right ear, which allowed me to face the staircase and anyone arriving by way of it.

More than once, between visits, I made myself pick up the telephone to call her, and was always relieved to find nobody home.

A month went by. Four weeks of a couple of days each in which I never tired of the lopsided company I kept. Even after the noises stopped, which sometimes they did, I never thought of knocking. The only faces I saw were the ones I passed on the stair, going or coming; the faces of strangers that, I realized, were more familiar to me now than Claire's face. Every afternoon I arrived, expecting the security system to have been fixed and the door to the building to stand closed in my face. But the only thing that changed in a month was the *Reader's Digest.* A slim, picture Bible took its place as the door prop.

What ended it was that the red door opened. But not from the inside, as I expected. I was crouched, with my usual ear to the wood, almost lulled to sleep by the familiar voices from within. I had time to see her coming and time to be utterly confused by her appearance here, when I knew she was in there. I had almost forgotten quite what she looked like.

"Hello, Franny." She was tired, using the bannister to help her. My head was pressed against her door. "What a surprise," she said. "What a fine surprise. How long have you been here?"

Without waiting for an answer she squatted down next to me and hugged me as hard as she had the last time I'd seen her.

"About a month," I told her. I knew I didn't have to. I could lie. I could stretch the truth. "I've been here about a month."

She unlocked the door and led me inside and there I confessed all. But before I began, Claire crossed the room and turned off her small tape machine, which was the source of all the noises of love I'd been listening to for weeks.

"That's whale music," she said. "I've been playing it every day since I met you, I don't know why."

She worked evenings in a museum, setting up exhibits. She left a little before five every afternoon, so I had missed her each time by only a few minutes. She hadn't been aware she left the music on until I told her.

"My god, what a thing you are!" she said when I had finished my story. "I never dreamed you were shy."

"It had nothing to do with shyness, Claire." I blushed. "I just didn't want to disturb you."

"You must have thought we were inexhaustible!"

"Just very punctual," I said. She was laughing and then I was laughing, and she came over and hugged me again and brushed back the hair from my face and looked hard at me. "Mmm," she said.

"Mmm, what?"

"I'm glad I played hooky today. You know, I was on my way to work and I got as far as the subway station and said to hell with it and turned around."

"Why?"

"I didn't have a cent on me. I didn't have a token. Someone had just thrown up going through the turnstile and I took that for my omen."

"It makes perfect sense!"

"Thank you, though the real reason is that I was up

all morning talking to my past, and I'm in no condition to hang paintings."

"I'll go away," I offered. I hated the thought.

"I'll kill you if you go away," she said.

Her apartment was a tiny room, higher than it was wide, with bare floors and a rough, vaulted ceiling of unhidden beams. "When I look up, I feel like I'm looking at the muscles of this building," she told me. I was as excited as a kid, arriving from a childhood of plush carpets and overstuffed chairs. I had grown up thinking of furniture as an exhibit, or a good way to hide the pee stains of years of terriers that spotted an expensive rug. My family's—or my mother's—idea of comfort was a kind of plumped up environment of pillows and sofas and fatly upholstered loveseats. But here, in Claire's loft, I hurt my bones sitting down, and loved it. Crossing the floor I was aware of the sharp, outdoor clack of my brown, tie shoes.

She called it her bungalow, no doubt trying to squeeze some sense of the country out of all the surrounding cityness. In fact, there was a rural feeling about the place, at least until you looked four stories down into the truck-honking, dolly-wheeling mayhem of Thompson Street. The windows were high and narrow, like church windows, letting in a thin, compromised light. There were three of them, and they were her mark upon the place, I thought, though they had lived here forever and she for only eleven months. But they came to remind me of her, the way they stood up sparsely and eloquently, letting in none of the outside world when they were closed, but easy enough to coax open.

The room had the sweet musty smell of beeswax and sandalwood, which surprised me until I remembered Claire over coffee at Hamburger Heaven, assuring me she never smoked at home. A standing lamp in one corner gave off a gray light by which I saw what I thought to be an old-fashioned stove, and next to that a refrigerator. Pushed up against the refrigerator, a desk, which you had to leap over to get to the bed. Bed and desk were practically interchangeable—both old doors supported by sturdy wooden crates. The bed had a thin mattress on it, covered by a sheet and quilt. The desk was covered with books. There was no desk chair, there was only a stool in front of the stove, and I imagined Claire standing her full height, scribbling, Thomas Wolfe–style, on top of the refrigerator. What furniture there was was crowded into one half of the room, away from the windows, to give Claire what she called the promise of space. The walls were white and bare. A black-handled broom stood up straight in one corner. There were no knickknacks anywhere. The only object whose place in it all I didn't understand was a rosewood Buddha, a statue the size of a grapefruit, sitting on the windowsill.

"I had to move the stove out to make room for the Siren," said Claire.

"The siren?"

She laughed. "With a capital 's,' though when I play it, it sounds more like the other. My piano, Franny. Have you ever really loved what you can't have?" I shook my head. "Well, I love the piano, only I have no talent for it."

She went to it, raised the cover and touched the keys, too lightly to make a sound. It was a real piano, a black, stand-up Wurlitzer with claw-and-ball feet that stopped looking like a stove to me the moment my friend put her hands on it. "Play something," I said. "Please play something, Claire."

"I'll do a waltz, but I warn you, Franny, I only play great music very badly."

This was true. I knew little or nothing about music, but even so I knew her performance would have horrified Strauss, whose "Blue Danube" she played. This didn't stop her, which at first I loved. Three times she started over because her hands bungled the beginning, and bungled badly even when she was well into the piece. "Botched!"

she yelled as she played. "Botched again!" she sang out her mistakes. "Too late to go back!" she finally cried after the third try, and kept on, jarring the peace and quiet of that small room until the tension hummed louder in my ears than the music. I was almost sweating as it ended.

"There!" said Claire.

She turned around on the piano stool. The only thing I could think to say was, "I never took piano lessons."

She was clearly amused. "Well, guess what? Neither did I."

"I took riding lessons," I said. I was sitting on Claire's bed, terribly aware of her watching me. "But the horses scared me to death."

"You don't have to be scared of me," she said softly, so softly I told myself I didn't hear what I heard.

"What horses did for most little girls, swimming in the ocean did for me," I went on.

"I'd like to hear about it." Claire got up, opened the refrigerator. I could see inside it from where I was sitting. There was nothing on the two bottom shelves, but on the top shelf, between a bottle of burgundy and an uncovered platter of spaghetti, sat the telephone. It was a white desk phone, and its cord lay on top of the spaghetti, like more spaghetti.

"Did you know it's soundproof?" she asked.

"What's soundproof?"

"The icebox." I shook my head. "Well, I didn't either. I mean, how would you? You don't spend time inside one to know."

"What's the phone doing in there, Claire?"

"It's preserving my sanity. It's allowing me to be a hermit."

I remembered her generous warning the day we met: Here's the phone number, it won't do you any good. I had wondered why she was so strangely hard to get hold of.

"I call out on it, but I hate the damn noise it makes,

13

and around here they catch up with you if you disconnect it or leave it off the hook. This is the only place I can't hear it ring. Unless the icebox door's open. Once I was getting some milk and the moment I touched the bottle the phone rang."

"What happened?"

"I dropped the bottle. It broke. Milk went everywhere."

"Did you ever try that again?"

"Try what?"

"Touching a milk bottle to see if the phone would ring?"

"No. I never did." Claire laughed, and I laughed with her.

The only food in the refrigerator besides the wine and pasta were some Brussels sprouts rolling loose in the vegetable drawer. Was I hungry? she wondered. There was stiff spaghetti. She could heat it up in a minute on the small campstove on the floor where she did all her cooking. We drank wine instead, sitting on Claire's bed—where else were we going to sit?—and I relaxed and told her what I'd never told anyone before, about the rush of waves that had tumbled me senseless, every childhood summer of my life.

"I called it body surfing, but it wasn't. Even as a very little girl I knew the smooth ride in on a breaker meant nothing to me if it didn't all come down on me at the end. I discovered it by mistake, Claire. The first time I didn't put myself out there to be tumbled, but after that, and especially when I got older, I'd do it every day sometimes. I'd desire it."

"Didn't anyone try to stop you?" asked Claire. "Didn't they wonder?" She was drinking wine from a mustard jar. I was drinking it cold from the bottle.

"You don't chill red, you know. White and rosé, yes, but never burgundy."

14

"Good," she said. "That means more room in the ice-box." She had been lying down and she raised herself on one elbow. "Answer me. Didn't they think you were some kind of odd child?"

"No. I don't know. They got used to it. They didn't really know what went on. It was always the same. My mother would see me flattened on the beach and come down from her umbrella and stand over me, blinking. She was sun sensitive and always forgot her dark glasses back up in the shade. I was breathing, she could see that. I'm sure I was smiling, and she could see that too. A few times, I remember, she tried to pull me away from the water, but that was all. After that she just flip-flopped back up to her umbrella and magazines and waited for lunch. Or supper."

"And your father?"

"My father hated sand, so all summer long he water-colored on the back porch of the beach cottage and cooked wild meals for us."

"Like what?"

"Like kidneys and coq au vin and sweetbreads and brains; all kinds of things."

"That's not so wild."

"Once he shucked five dozen oysters, Claire, *sixty* oysters! Imagine it! For the three of us! Of course I hated them. I was just a kid. And my mother was boycotting my father for teaching me the word 'aphrodisiac,' so she wouldn't touch them either."

"Good god!"

"So he ate them all. He must have stayed up all night to do it, which he did quite often anyway just to rest from the world. In the morning there was nothing but shells, and I helped him load the little red wagon full of them and together we towed it down to the beach. He rarely went on the beach. Whenever he did he went sockless, in his brown shoes, and he walked very carefully and was angry if he got sand in them."

"And he didn't think it was strange, this suicidal passion of yours? Was it suicidal, Franny? What did you think, going out to meet that huge wet thing? Was it there to kill you?"

"Oh, no! It was there to save me! There was nothing suicidal about it; I just wanted to forget everything for a few seconds, take a break, let something else do the thinking and working for a while." I laughed. "No, no. It was my deliverance. I was so self-conscious, Claire, even as a kid. I was thinking and watching myself all the time. And here I'd found a way to get really lost, that's all. It was like sex for me, I guess. I guess it was like being touched all over, all at once, by something that wanted nothing in return."

"Uh-huh. Yeah, I see. I rode horses. Same thing."

"Same big wedge between your legs, except under those waves it was everywhere. The power and force was coming from all directions, all at the same time. And do you know what it would sound like to me right before I landed on the beach? The sound the sea made leaving my ears and the shells made rubbing each other under the foam? It would sound to me like some soprano singing the word 'home.' No kidding. I was dazed and only half with it every time, but I swear that voice was singing 'home' at the top of its lungs. The first time it happened I was still quite a young kid, and I raised my head to look and see where that voice was coming from, that's how sure of it I was."

Claire was looking at me. "You're a beautiful child," she said. "You're a beautiful creature, Franny."

And I was. I knew I was. That night I could feel my beauty standing up inside me for the first time in my life. I took a late train home to New Jersey, using the black window beside me as my mirror. My thin face and neck, my brown hair cut square: I could have been a child—someone's little boy. But beautiful, yes. Someone had said so. And I could sit now with darkness on my side, erasing the tenements that crowded the track, and stare at this creature given back to me by the glass. And think nothing. Or think only of the next time I would see my friend. Our work was badly coordinated. I had nights free, she had days. She worked on weekend afternoons as well, but Saturday morning, she had said. Come Saturday morning.

"You'll be exhausted, Claire. You will have been up all night."

"Well, Sunday then." She had given in. I hadn't expected her to give in and I was disappointed.

That Sunday I went to see her, and the next, and in between I was restless, almost useless at work, though I said none of this to Claire and gave her only my calmest, "Oh, that will be better for you," when she told me she'd changed her workshift to days. The rest of February passed almost entirely in conversation. Three or four times a week we sat or lay on Claire's bed, clothes and coats on against the cold draft that leaked out of her wall heater. Sometimes we drank wine, a good bottle I'd taken from my parents' abundant cellar. Sometimes the music of the whales carried us from thought to thought. I did most of the talking, which seemed no injustice at the time. It was like seining a familiar river for the first time, a river I'd sailed across and rowed upon for years without knowing its depth or the variable surface of the river bottom. And in the first week of March, as these things not readily available to the eye became more and more clear to me, the surface became clouded, so I doubted all I'd ever known about my river and at times felt utterly solitary upon it.

"As far as our backgrounds go," Claire told me one day, "you and I aren't of the same egg, exactly, but part of the same omelette." It didn't matter so much that this was true or not, she said it to quell the loneliness our differences always caused me. This particular difference came up around sex.

That afternoon I had protested, only half seriously, "Claire, why is it the more you know about me the less I feel I know about you?"

She had laughed. "Because, dear Franny, you never ask."

"All right. Who was it who kept you from your sleep the day you caught me eavesdropping at your door? You said it was someone from your past. Was it a man?" Claire nodded. "Are you in love with him?"

"I love him," she said. "He's my brother. He gets in trouble from time to time and we talk for hours on the telephone."

"I see."

"You have a real demon, don't you, Franny?"

"A demon?"

"A jealous streak."

I nodded. "Don't you?"

"No."

"Not when you were younger?"

She laughed. "This is about as young as I've ever been." We were lying head to foot and she held my foot. "Farm kids don't have time to be kids; and I don't mean just the milking, ploughing, planting part of it. I mean that by the time you're old enough to walk yourself out to the barn, or out to the fields to pull thistles, you're already watching the mating, birthing, dying cycle at work. At six, you know too much to be a kid, and what's worse, if you're as Catholic as we were, you're made to feel guilty about imitating the animals long before your little body's even capable of such a thing."

I told her that dogs in the park had been my only learning ground. I remembered, when I was nine or ten, the sickening sight of a lap-size Lhasa Apso in heat, disappearing under the legs of two leashless Dobermans. This was my first public encounter with the sexual act. My mother was with me. She was leading me home from Mary Weissmuller's birthday party. I was chattering away about the afternoon's highlight, when Mary's grandfather, who used to play Tarzan in the movies, swung in on a rope.

"Well, dear, where in the world did he swing from?" my mother wanted to know, but I couldn't tell her. At that moment the only thing in the world for me was the sleek, muscled body of a Doberman, quickly joined by another, standing like a flesh wall in the path ahead of us. And rolling around on the ground beneath them, looking just like the stuffed animals I'd barely outgrown, lay the Lhasa Apso. Her feet were now under her, now up in the air, and the larger dogs took turns falling on her. Her little black tongue was out, as theirs were. Her owner, coming quickly on the scene with a plaid umbrella, was trying to get at her or her leash to drag her away. The whole episode couldn't have lasted more than a minute, and until the arrival of the owner it was almost entirely silent. I did remember one sound: the sound made by the dogs' toenails on the cement path. But that was all. Only my own mind imagined the screams of the little Lhasa Apso, and made certain they were screams of indignation rather than pleasure.

I finished the story and we were both quiet for a minute. Finally Claire said, "God, you've led a sheltered life." She shook her head. "That was a cruel thing to say. It's just that at nine or ten I was trying to unlearn what you at that age were just learning."

"Well, if I could have learned it any sooner I would have, Claire, but until a dog lies down in front of you on the path, you don't notice it."

"It doesn't matter," she shrugged. "Some people notice it. I noticed it and then I only wanted to unnotice it. It seems like you wanted to ignore the whole business from the start."

This was true. I was a magnificently late bloomer. If it had been my choice I would have holed up in childhood and never bloomed at all. As it was, my mind kept my body a kid's body until a few months before I met Claire, and even then the changes were slow and comically subtle. At twenty-two my breasts were flat as saucers; now at twenty-three they hugged my chest like teacups. I still did sit-ups every morning to keep my stomach flat and muscular as a Greek god's. I never had a period. There was no boy I loved. My face got me into the movies for twelve and under at almost twice that age. And all because I willed it that way.

"What were you afraid of?" asked Claire. It was the middle of winter. We lay in her bed together and she held my foot.

"When?"

"When you saw the dogs fucking?"

Nobody said "fucking" the way Claire did, with such disinterest.

"What was I afraid of?"

"Yeah."

"I don't know what I was afraid of. Of course, seeing something whomped on by something else; that was sad and it scared me. But in all this my mind was racing way ahead of my body, so I sensed things my body was still too young to know."

"Such as?"

"Such as there is no pleasure without pain."

"Oh, bullshit."

"You don't believe me? If my mind had been a kid's mind I would have passed those dogs, rooting for all three of them."

Claire had been leaning forward intently, and now she slumped back against the pillows at the other end of the bed. "You don't know what you're talking about," she said. "It's all academic to you, isn't it? You don't have to answer this, you know that, but I'm going to ask it anyway. I've got this wild idea you're still a virgin, aren't you?" She shook her hand at me. "Now wait. If you're going to say something don't say it until I tell you first how exotic you are to me, virgin or not. You're just not like other children of the Fifties. You're a beauty. You're a rare, intelligent bird."

But there wasn't anything I was about to say. I was no longer in the room. My mind flew out the tall, clear windows of Claire's apartment, down to the docks and across the Hudson River. It flew down the turnpike, past the evil-smelling factories and incinerators, and off into the deep grass and greener miles of New Jersey. It returned to summer, to familiar flower and vegetable gardens. It stepped cautiously over a ground cover of lush poison ivy; a hidden homeplate in a grown-over baseball diamond. It turned, and there at the back door of a square, white house stood Britta the cook, her hairnet strung haphazardly as a cobweb across her rapidly thinning hair. But she wasn't holding her arms out to me, she was shaking flour from her white apron. She put the apron on again and her plump hands scolded her thighs, beating a thin cloud of tomorrow's cake up into the air around her head until she sneezed.

"Kerchoo!" Claire shook, then held herself ready for the next one which never came. "You went off for a while," she said, blowing her nose into a white handkerchief she'd pulled from her parka pocket. It was a cold night and she'd wrapped the quilt around our legs.

"I went to where it was warm," I said. "A little daydream about a hairnet."

I didn't visit Claire for a few days after that. What I was waiting for wasn't clear to me until in a flurry of fish and singing budgies and one fat albino hamster whirling round and round on his squeaky wheel, I heard her voice. She called me at the pet shop. We'd never talked on the telephone before.

"Your voice is deep," I said. "I love it. Has it always been this deep?"

"You're whispering," she laughed.

I watched the blur of colors in a fishbowl become a man's face as he stood up from behind the glass. "Do we always talk like this?"

"Like what?" she asked.

"Like we mean every word?"

"I think so."

"Claire?"

"Mmm?"

"This is the first time we've been in public together since the day we met."

"I guess that's true," she laughed again. "How do we look?"

There was a pause. "We look like we're very close," I said.

"But you've been hiding from me, Fran."

I shook my head for emphasis, though of course she couldn't see it. "Oh no, Claire. I've been waiting for you. It was your turn to come to me."

"It was my turn to come to you," she said, "and here I am."

She had something to give me, and after work I rushed down to Thompson Street and arrived out of breath at her door. She was there with her arms out to pull me to her. She was beaming. What she wanted to give me was a haircut, and I let her. The scissors were paper-cutting scissors. Her only mirror was a small pocket mirror with a hole in the center that Claire said was for signaling airplanes. As she worked she warned me she'd never done this to anyone before, and when she was through I looked in the mirror once, closed my eyes and wailed.

"Oh, Franny, it can't be all that terrible." She put her chin against my neck and looked in the mirror too. The signal hole in the center took away her right eye and my left one. "It's a close cut," she said. "You weren't expecting a close cut?"

The hair, what was left of it, stood out from my scalp in uneven patches, some an inch long, some closer to two inches. Claire stood back from me for a moment. She nodded. "I was afraid when I started. Usually that means a very good thing will come of it. But it's awful, you're right. It looks like some kind of cockeyed agriculture. Like only half the farmers fertilized their soil."

And before I could stop her she was back in there again with the scissors, going at it with the same exuberant stubbornness I'd seen her use to butcher Strauss. She worked madly, with no method that I could understand, though most of this time I kept my eyes squeezed shut and only knew what I knew of her in silky waves, each time she passed a hand across my head. I think she hypnotized me that night. The haircut seemed to go on for hours. By the time she laid down the scissors and peeled back the collar of my coat to brush the hair clippings from my neck, it was late. And she didn't brush them, she blew them. She pushed my head slightly forward and blew a long, warm wind across my skin.

"Do you want to keep this?" she asked. She had a small ball of my hair in her hand. "It's so fine, like a baby's hair, Franny. You know you've missed the last train to New Jersey?"

I nodded, then shook my head, and she put the hair in her pocket. I didn't go home that night. I didn't go home for more than a week after that. My parents kept a small apartment on the West Side, and this is where I headed from Thompson Street. Claire wrapped a scarf around my neck, and before I left she pulled me to her by the two ends of the scarf and kissed me. It wasn't just a friend's kiss, though it was more the affectionate kiss of a child than a lover. I don't remember how I kissed her back, or if I did, or whether this was the first time we kissed, or if we'd been kissing, in our way, since the day we met.

"Come see me," she said, and let me go. In the subway station I caught sight of myself, one half of my face at a time, in a thin mirror beside a cosmetic machine. I didn't know who I saw, some older self with a small furred head and mouth half open in surprise, cheeks and forehead almost feverishly bright. It was as if Claire with her scissors had taken me down to my bones—inside my bones where I was animal and holy and now suddenly afraid of being either or both. I turned back to her. I remembered the ball of hair in her pocket, like a delicate web of who I'd been. I pushed through the turnstile and climbed the stairs to the street, and walked until I could see her dark and curtainless windows. I raised both my arms to her in case she was looking out at me, then hurried back down underground to catch my train.

2

If two Dobermans and a Lhasa Apso woke me from childhood, it's possible a withered arm pushed me into adult life. Or pulled me. Or at least waved me on.

Claire and I were discussing Eden, lying down one evening side by side on her bed. We had a hill of blankets on top of us, and all our clothes on underneath that. Outside, a blizzard was busy dumping a foot of snow on New York City.

"What do good Catholics think of the serpent?" I asked her.

"He's the devil," she answered, "though to me that's never meant much. I couldn't believe in horns and a tail any more than I could believe in white robes and haloes. Even as a kid, I saw colors and shapes when anyone said the word God. I knew people who looked the way God does in the picture Bibles, and they weren't any more like

25

him than I was. Also, it seemed crazy that he was a he."

"Well, what was the serpent to you then? Just an old rattlesnake caught in a tree?"

"What was the serpent to me? To me, Franny, the serpent was, or at least is now in my mature thinking, a voyeur."

"A voyeur?"

"Yes. Someone spellbound by the destiny of others. The eyes at the window. The clubfoot of God."

"What do you mean, the clubfoot of God?" I was used to having to reach way out to make the connections that seemed so logical to Claire, but there were still some that escaped me.

"I mean that the serpent or the voyeur is in all of us, just as God, whatever that means, is in all of us. But the voyeur is the meaner side of God."

"Meaner?"

"Well, more base. More common. The part of God that's tied to the earth. Like a clubfoot."

"Nothing lofty."

"Right. And often having rotten intentions. You see, Franny, the voyeur has all God's eyesight, but he can see best in the dark. He's at home in the alleys, crouching behind garbage cans, scaring old ladies. The shadows excite him. Mystery excites him. Every stray dog is his ally, and every dusk is his friend. He's reptilian, almost. If I had to classify him evolutionwise, I'd stick him with the dinosaurs—the one that survived. But for all his dim living, the occasional bedroom light does attract him, for one reason."

"What's that?"

"It softens his heart. It melts him. Under the glow of it he thinks of bonfires and a time when he was nothing but warm." Claire was laughing now. "I swear, Franny, I get going with you and then I find myself believing what comes out of my mouth." She looked straight at me, serious

26

again. "And neither of us should have to believe that. I want to let my mind go more and more astray."

"Oh, Claire, you *are* astray. You live in your imagination almost all the time we're together."

She rolled on her side and propped her head so she was looking down at me. "What do you mean by that?"

"You make this world," I said, "and you invite me into it."

"Do you like that? or does it seem the only way I can be with you is to turn it all into a play that we're standing outside of, looking in on?"

"I'm not looking in on anything, Claire, and neither are you. Are you?"

"I don't know."

"I don't think you are. I think you're spinning the imaginary world out from you, out from us, so we're wrapped inside it, completely caught up in it, not outside it at all."

"Well, what's it like for you when you leave here?" she asked. "What happens to that world then?"

I closed my eyes and tried to remember every detail of thought and feeling from the last time Claire had walked me to the subway. For some reason it didn't frighten me to ride the trains at night, even though Claire thought it was a terrible idea and offered me a sleeping bag and a spot on her floor. Or in her bed. That's what she'd offered me two nights before, one arm in her parka, the other about to be, turning around for a second with her back to the red front door. It was after midnight, and I shook my head. Afterward, we walked the four flights down without saying a word. "Awareness of the thinness of walls," was what Claire usually called our descending silence, though this time it had nothing to do with that.

On the street she took my arm and didn't let go of it. In the subway station there were a number of nameless and shapeless characters sleeping upright on the green benches, and one policeman tapping his billy club lightly across his palm. "I don't want to let you go," she whispered. "Daniel to the lions."

"They only eat the weak of heart," I told her. "You have nothing to worry about."

But how did I feel, not so much seeing as sensing the subway doors closing in front of me, because I was too aware, all of a sudden, of the intensity of Claire's face beyond them? It was as if that face was all that was left, hovering on the platform as the train began its slow lurch forward. She had the widest eyes in that moment. She had a longing I could almost feel the heat of. Or at least that's the way I understood her look, and then her hand that had held my arm came up in a hesitant wave that matched the awkwardness of motion of the vanishing subway.

Where had the world gone then? How long had I carried her with me? I hadn't stood between the cars to let the noisy updraft lift her out of my mind. I had sat, very conscientiously I thought, next to an elderly woman reading a Russian newspaper and not far from a policeman. The ride uptown had been uneventful, and I felt neither relief nor disappointment. I wasn't completely of the world of my surroundings. I never could be after a visit to Claire. It had been this way the first time we met and it was this way now, almost three months later.

"I don't really leave here," I told her, opening my eyes to her own wide ones looking down on me. The intensity was all over her face again, seeming to expand it. "I live in your world all the time now. A few people have noticed."

This was true. My parents worried less that I was now spending all my time in the city than that I seemed "aloof," as my mother put it, or "calm" according to my father, whenever I called home to talk to them.

Claire was relieved. Her body, running the length of mine in the bed, relaxed. It was as if all the clothes she was wearing suddenly loosened around her. She pushed the short hair back from my forehead. She cupped her palm to my chin and I watched her lips almost do something or say something, then decide against it. It was a funny, transparent moment that left both of us open for anything, and when nothing happened it was impossible to know who felt more responsible for the loss.

"Listen," said Claire, pulling her hand away to bring the blankets up closer around us. And we were back in the Garden of Eden again, as if we'd never left there for the worlds of memory and possibility. "The serpent's not even the central character in all this, you know that don't you, Franny?"

I nodded. "But I still don't get his part in it," I said. "I thought he was the tempter, and you're telling me he was just some old voyeur, some spectator, which would make him not the cause of anything at all."

"Ha!" Claire practically shouted. "That's it. You just said it. He's not the cause of anything, at least nothing as earth-shaking as the Fall of Man."

"Yeah, well I guess to put that all on one little snake—"

"Unh-unh," she shook her head. "The point is you've got to give Eve credit."

"Credit for what?"

"For putting her jaws around that apple. Face it, that serpent could never have talked a log into eating a piece of fruit, forbidden or not. Eve was responsible for the first bite, and for every bite after that—except Adam's. He was responsible for his own, just as she was. And that old voyeur just sat in the top of his tree and watched it all roll downhill from there." She stopped herself. "Not downhill. I don't believe that." She smiled. "I guess I never was a very good Catholic. You see, as soon as you put everyone in charge of their own self, so none of it falls back on the devil, or Eve, or on God, so God's just your own self, the you of you, it seems you have a brighter world, not a bleaker one. Whatever went on in exile after humankind swallowed the bait, I bet it was more humbling, more frightening, more daring than anything Paradise could offer. I bet it was more exciting—hell, I know this is more exciting than anyone's idea of heaven."

She was all lit up and practically flying out of the bed, laughing as she said this. "Christ, Franny. Those two didn't even hold hands until Paradise became the ordinary world."

"Which two?"

"Eve and Adam. In the paintings you see them before the bite, and nothing. They don't even look affectionate. But after it, they're standing together, or fleeing hand in hand, fig leaves streaming off them, and they're really feeling something, you can tell."

"Sure," I said, "but are they feeling for each other or are they just feeling terrible about the situation? Masaccio's got this painting, very bare and simple, of Adam and Eve leaving the Garden, and I've never seen such anguish on a human face. They aren't happy, Claire."

"I know that painting," she said, "but who said anything about happy? At least they're feeling something, aren't they? At least they're alive. Heaven is just where it's safe, Franny, and who the hell wants to spend a life in that kind of heaven?"

Saying this, she got up, climbed over the desk and moved to the dark windows. For the first time in that quiet, I could hear the snow hitting the panes in a windblown volley. I watched Claire kneel and pick up the binoculars she kept on the sill. Instinctively, she looped the strap around her neck and raised them to eye level. She leaned into them. Her elbows were planted on the sill. I heard her sigh deeply as if to erase all talk, all words from her body. Then suddenly she caught her breath, and still facing out into the night she whispered, "Franny. Come quickly."

"What is it?" I asked.

"There's a man across the way making love to a woman."

I wasn't sure what I'd heard.

"There's a man . . . I can't see through all this damn snow, but there's at least a very large part of a man. . . ."

Claire started laughing. I came over and crouched down next to her in front of the window. Below us, Thompson Street lay without traffic or people. The only movement was a regular march of snowdrifts up and down what would have been the middle of the street. Even the plow hadn't gotten through yet, though we could hear its low-pitched whine from somewhere else in the neighborhood.

There was an eerie color to everything, an almost green-white, as if our part of the city were living for a few hours in the light of a giant television set. There was something, though—a yellow square hung up like a Japanese lantern on the face of the apartment building directly across from Claire's. This was the fourth-story window whose light had attracted her. The snow distorted everything, blurred and magnified everything, so now when I looked out to see what had set her laughing, I felt, for a second, I was in the room with what I watched.

"Oh," I said. "Oh my."

The snow slowed down for us and suddenly we could see clearly through it. Across the street, a horizontal man, visible from waist to knee, appeared and disappeared at rhythmic intervals inside the frame of the lit-up window.

"That," said Claire, "is the biggest ass I've ever seen."

Even in profile, his buttocks were enormous. They rose and fell at a pace that exhausted us both. We passed the binoculars back and forth for a few minutes, then set them down because neither of us needed to be any closer to what we saw. The snow had let up, though the clouds still hugged the tops of the buildings.

"Do you think this is nasty?" she said.

I nodded. "I'm sure it is."

"It feels less creepy without the binoculars."

As we watched, a body paler than the buttocks began to appear in the bottom of the window frame, under the trunk of the man.

"There she is," whispered Claire. "She's a skinny thing." We could only see a thin stripe of her running the length of the man. He had one arm wrapped around the small of her back. Whichever way he moved, he was bringing her with him.

"I wish we could see her face." Now I was whispering too.

"No, no, Franny. It's much better this way. I like them both without heads. We can give them whatever faces we want them to have."

"You mean we can make them Masaccios?"

"Or faces more in love with what they're doing."

Claire stood up. I could feel her watching me. A minute went by. In their world across the street nothing had changed, or at least nothing we could see. Perhaps the sweat gleamed more brightly on their bodies, but we were too far away to notice.

"I wonder how noisy they are," she said. "A thing is so much less awesome when one of the senses is taken away. And the smell of it . . . I wonder if she uses perfume. I wonder what the smell of that's turned to now. Franny!" She was groping for the binoculars. I stood up against her, trying to see what she saw. The couple was upright now, and he was stroking the side of her. His right arm still pressed her to him at the small of her back.

"They're done," I said. "Thank god. It's about time."

"They're not done."

At that point the woman must have climbed up onto the bed because suddenly the entire window was taken up with her waist and hips and legs. She was facing us first, then facing away. She was a skinny woman in every place but her thighs.

"She's doing a little dance to please him," said Claire.

"Or to please herself."

"Can you stand this, Franny?"

"I think it's funny."

"You didn't see him the way I just saw him. Look through here." She gave me the binoculars. "Do you notice something wrong?"

He was trying to catch her and pull her down to him, like a man fishing the sky. I saw his chest—it was a huge chest—and then he turned and I saw the thick, loose flesh of his shoulders and back. She was still dancing on the bed, and he reached his left arm up as if to claw her the length of her body. She grabbed the arm and pushed it away, not roughly as I would have expected, her little strength against his, and suddenly I saw that it was a child's arm on a grown man. It was thin and oddly lumpy, as if it had been broken in a dozen places. The wrist was cocked forward and frozen that way, at a right angle. The hand itself looked like a hoof, with fingers and thumb so balled up they seemed to stop at the knuckles. As I watched the arm's slow fall from the woman's body, I had the strange sensation of being lied to.

"It's spooky, isn't it?" said Claire. She took the binoculars from me. "If the other arm were like that he could be some kind of dinosaur."

"Tyrannosaurus Rex," I nodded, "or Iguanodon. They were all built that way, for running, not for loving."

Bare-eyed, we both looked across the street for the last time, just at the moment the withered arm seemed to fill the window with itself. Claire shivered. "Maybe he's very kind to her," she said. "Maybe he gives her just what she wants."

At that, a healthy arm, hers or his it was impossible to tell, snapped down the shade that had been waiting to fall on this anonymous encounter, and I was blinded for a few seconds by the absence of artificial light.

"Come here," said Claire, out of the silence. She was still shivering. I was standing so close to her our sides and our shoulders touched.

"I *am* here," I said.

"Here." She turned me and pressed me against her. My nose was at her neck, smelling something neither sweet nor sour—more like earth or dust. The sleeve of her parka was loud in my ears as she rubbed my hair up from the neck, against the grain. "Your head's like a little sleeping owl, Franny." I could feel the warm circles of her breath on my scalp.

"Are you frightened?" she asked.

"Of you? Of this?"

Through the top of my head I could feel her cheek muscles smiling. "No. Of the scene across the street. I thought it might be like the time you saw the dogs fucking."

I pushed my head away from her so I could look up at her. "I was a kid then, Claire. I was nine years old. I was still coloring with those fat crayons and sitting on my daddy's lap. You think I don't know how babies are born? You think I'm some kind of goddess? I'm no goody-goody."

"I'm not calling you a goody-goody, Franny. The most I'm calling you is naïve."

"Naïve? Why? Just because I don't go out and get laid every night and keep the shades up while I'm doing it?"

"What's that got to do with . . . ?"

"Just because I'm a skinny little thing with no tits, no hips, no ass. Just because you gave me this monk's haircut that may never grow out? Just because I still live with my parents from time to time, and they aren't divorced and never have been, and don't plan to be, and they love me, and I can stand them? What does it take not to be naïve in this world, Claire? I'm more streetwise than anyone you've ever known. I'm a world traveler. I've been across the ocean. I know how to spend money or save it. I can

34

order food in French, for god's sake, or Italian, or Russian. What's so goddamn naïve about that?"

"Franny . . . !"

Claire was trying to calm me but I wouldn't let her. She wouldn't let go of me completely. She held me strongly by the shoulders. Her face was startled and amused at the same time, which infuriated me. "You think it's a joke!" I told her. "You think I'm a little fool. What's gotten into you tonight, Claire? Why are you so much better than me all of a sudden? Is it what we saw? Did that dinosaur give you a thrill, poor jerk with a withered arm? Or the woman? Of course, it was the woman, her little dance on the bed. You loved that, didn't you? The biologist in you must love watching beasts in the wild. You're the serpent, Claire. You're the real voyeur. Sex is a spectator sport to you, isn't it? *Isn't* it? Christ, we've been lying in bed together for more than a month now and you haven't even touched me! You haven't even taken off my coat!"

"You little monster," she said. "You poor forgetful child."

"Don't call me a child!" I was trying to shake her off but she was a grown woman, bigger and stronger than I was, with years of heavy farm equipment and balky livestock in her blood.

"I don't mind your insults, Franny, I don't mind your anger, but let me set the facts straight for you." She had moved her hands from my shoulders to right above my elbows. She was squeezing me hard. "We've been lying in bed because my spinster life doesn't happen to include chairs. I haven't taken off your coat because it's too damn cold in here, and I assumed you, a college-educated young woman of sound mind and body, could, if your heart desired it, do away with your own coat and mine, too, for that matter. I'm not your Lancelot. I'm not your Charlton Heston. I'm not even your suave young Moondoggie pad-

35

dling out to save Gidget from the arms of the seaweed. Get this, Franny." She was talking right into my face. "If you expect me to seduce you, throw you down, smother you with kisses, leap all over your body, you'll be disappointed. I offered you my bed—to sleep in, not just to talk in—two nights ago, remember?" She shook me. *"Remember?"* I quickly nodded. I did remember. "If you want me, you're going to have to come halfway to get me. Otherwise on your part it's just you wanting the idea of me, isn't it? It's a put-on boldness, nothing to do with you."

In the dim light of the window, this was the first time I noticed her scar. It was thin and faint, running the back side of her cheek near the hairline. I remember thinking when I saw it, Now we've started something; now we're really taking each other in. I nodded my head at it because she still held both my arms. "I've never seen that before," I told her.

"And what is there in you I've never seen before, you little mystery?" She put two fingers on my lips. "I'll find it. Don't tell me. I'll figure it out."

But we weren't made tender by a few words. There was a momentary truce between us that neither of us trusted. I could never come easily out of my anger because I put so much of myself into it to begin with. Claire let go of me and lit a candle by the bed. In the light of it I saw what I thought must be her true face, though later that night when I saw her true face it looked nothing like this. She looked old to me for the first time, and if there was any single thing that softened me toward her, melted my anger, it was her age. I had the same sense as when I first met her: It was an honor to have been chosen by her.

"How can I make it easier for you, Franny?" she asked. She was sitting cross-legged on the bed.

"For one thing, take your hands out of those stupid pockets and undress me."

She smiled. She was surprised. "Okay. I'll light the wall heater first."

"I didn't think you had any heat in here."

"Just this miserable old spitter of soot which I've never had a good enough reason to use until now."

One match and the heater exploded like a bellows. The warm draft blew Claire's hair forward from her shoulders. Two flakes of soot stuck to her forehead. I saw all of this in candlelight as she came toward me on the bed. Beyond that light was the milky-green light of the blizzard, which had started up again. Both lights were in the room. Both lights gave off light. She was first in the green light, then in the gold. Her hands were shining, perfect. They were green and rough and long, and the bones stood out from them.

She put both her palms on my cheeks and pressed in. Her fingers must have felt my brain working, my teeth chattering, though no longer with the cold. She massaged my cheeks as she held them, and I felt the sudden warmth of her—not just her skin, but all her organs, leaping through her calloused thumbs. I had a wild urge to tear her out of her clothes before she put a hand on mine. I grabbed her sleeves and she came down with them, willingly, her whole long body easing onto mine.

"Oh, you do want me," she said. She whispered it. One of her legs was across me on the bed. She sat up then and took my coat off and into her arms. The way she held it, it had all the weight and substance of a body.

I lay and let her peel my clothes away until I was only in my shirt and underpants, feeling suddenly all bones and awkward on top of the covers. Claire was slowly unbuttoning me. She slipped her hands in over my shoulders and down around the undersides of my breasts. "Beautiful shoulders," she said. "Beautiful breasts. I thought I'd cry, Franny, I really did, if I got through all those coats and

37

sweaters and under the last layer there was nothing but air."

"There isn't much," I said.

"There's more than you know."

She was moving slowly, unbuttoning slowly. She took me in with a calm curiosity I'd never expected from a moment like this. She never took the one hand from me. She stroked my face and neck, my breasts again, the hard muscles of my belly. And the whole time she talked to me, saying I don't remember what. She whispered to my body parts; like a good doctor, she told me where she would touch me next. The unbuttoning hand eased me out of my shirt and moved to join the other one at the top elastic of my underpants. "I'm going to move down now, Franny." She hesitated, then her hand cupped my thigh, all the way up where the softness becomes a bone. She was sighing deeply. Her eyes were closed as if she were trying very hard to remember what to do next. I suddenly wanted her to hurry as she moved her second hand down. I wanted her to shout, not to whisper: "If Eve had known places like this, sweet being, she would never have thought twice about the apple."

I understood that she was talking to calm me, the way you would calm a horse. Later I realized that she had been talking as much to calm herself; that her slowness or awkwardness of passion wasn't for my benefit—to demonstrate our equality—but as real in her as a kind of sexual heat was in me, though at the time I couldn't have known or guessed this about myself. First scenes are so poignantly passionate in so many ways afterward, but at the time there is always one part of you frozen, or screaming to stop; if not out of fear then out of not wanting this first scene gone and behind you, but ahead of you still. In me the voice that rang loudest that night, lying in only my underpants on the blankets of Claire's bed, was not the soprano of the waves chanting *home,* but another, almost muscular voice assuring me that a woman could never really lose anything to a woman; that even after this, I would still have my first scene ahead of me. There was something about a woman's bed and a woman's hand on my thigh that didn't count.

But Claire knew none of my thoughts, though god knows, her own internal voices were surely loud enough that night to burn her ears. I saw it in her eyes. She kept blinking them, as if to swallow what she saw. I imagined then that taking in enough of what surrounded her was the only defense she had against her mind's chatter. Which is why that night, preparing to be my lover, she studied me as a scientist would, filling her head with every detail of my skin.

Still in her coat and clothes, still with her hands between my thighs, she stood up in front of me, bent over, her loose hair darkening half her face. "I may be losing courage," she whispered. She straightened her lips in a queer smile. "It's never just emotion the first time with anyone, Franny. It's courage and emotion and luck, and not much skill of any kind. Curiosity's part of it, and there's something daredevil in it. If I take off my clothes now and climb into bed with you, it will change us, you know that, don't you?" I nodded. "And you know I'm a woman, and you have to want that too. It can't just be me wanting it. I didn't think this through before I got you down to your little underpants. But you do the next thing now. It's yours. You're Eve, too, remember. There are your clothes," she nodded at the pile on the floor, "and here I am in mine."

So I did the next thing. I took off my underpants. She was all zipped up and buttoned, and I was naked, feeling soft-headed in the billowing heat. She had loved how many women before she loved me? and she was asking me to take care of her.

It's a strange thing not to know how to touch. I had told myself over and over again, through years of solitary living, that I knew as well as anyone else how to give pleasure and receive it, because I was the same animal they were. But the mechanics are tricky. Even the simplest maneuvers seem designed to trip you up. Luckily, by the time I got down to unfastening her bra, Claire was ready to break the long, lonely silence. She burst out laughing. I was working so hard at the hooks she had only half her circulation.

"Ow, Franny, you're killing me. Don't yank it like that; it stretches. Just give it a little slack and it'll come apart."

"I've never been up close to one of these before."

"Here," she said, reaching her own hands around so her shoulder blades humped up like wings. "I'll help you the first time."

Once her clothes were out of the way I expected something huge and warm to enfold us both, like the muse of lovemaking, or at least a good angel. It wasn't disinterest I felt, pulling her undressed body down next to mine on the bed, but it certainly wasn't what I thought passion would be. It was closest to compassion, and friendliness, no different with our clothes on or off. What was different was how soft she was. Her skin against mine made me catch my breath, which made her laugh and hug me closer.

"The softness surprised me the first time too," she said. "It still surprises me."

"It's like a sheep's foot," I said.

"What is?"

"Between the two halves of a sheep's hoof it's as soft as this. I dragged a lamb off the road once and sat for a long time and touched it where I knew I'd never be able to touch it if it were alive."

"Franny!"

"No, it's true. I never imagined I'd find a place on anyone as soft as that."

I was smoothing the back of her knee with my palm. She was lying curled on her side, taking me in, taking in

all of my boniness without touching me. She was memo-
rizing me, I was certain, and I see now that that was her
gentlest way of having me. She was loving me so carefully
I should have been flattered, but I wanted her to be rough.
I wanted to force her out of herself, force her to come to
me. Why wouldn't she leap off into the wildness I had
imagined to be sexual love?

She was waiting, lying now with her arms up over her
head, shifting to her back, uncurling. I had never seen her
body beneath her clothes. It was covered with fine, light
hairs, thicker in her armpits and in the dark triangle of
her crotch. Her skin was pale. Her breasts were a woman's
breasts, full and pale around the dark brown of her nipples. I forgot what her face looked like. She held it back
in shadow. Her hair was invisible, the same dark as the
darkness. I could feel her watching me and I could feel
her body waiting.

She whispered, "Go ahead, Franny. Don't think about
what to do, just do it." One arm came down, and on the
way she wet her finger with saliva. She opened her legs.
For a second I could see the oval of flesh half hidden by
her pubic hair, and then she buried her finger there.

Her body kept coming up to meet her fingers. She
was touching herself with two fingers now, holding herself
open with the other hand and moving her fingers in slow
circles, smaller and smaller, the little jumps of her thighs
and belly coming faster and faster. Of course I knew this,
I knew how a woman gave herself pleasure, how I had
always given myself pleasure. But I sat now like a stranger
between her knees. I was a stranger. My hands were dumb
things that suddenly belonged no more to me than to the
man behind the shade across the street. I imagined him
again, pawing his woman, and in my mind I replaced Claire's
own arm, working and rocking in front of me, with his
withered one.

I don't know how close she was to orgasm. I erased

41

her body and heard only the short, familiar panting of something animal coming from her throat. I took her arm and twisted it away from her. She had her fingers inside her and they came out with a sharp sucking sound. "Oh, don't," she said. It was no more than an exhale. Her body jerked up from the waist so her face was close to mine when she said it again.

The words snapped something in me and I suddenly saw her, saw her true face. And in it I imagined all the anguish of Masaccio's Eve.

I released her arm and lowered her back to the bed, and wished I had something to cover us with. I put her parka on her. She lay with her eyes closed, her bare legs crossed and hanging off the bed. "Come be with me," she whispered, patting the covers beside her. "Whoever you are, come down here and be with me."

There was no sound except inside my own head. I could feel Claire breathing against my cheek. I could see the candlelight changing shape and color as the flame burned taller, then died in a pool of wax. I didn't expect anything or want anything, even after the voices in me backed away to an inarticulate blur. I felt exhausted. Claire had one arm across me and one arm under my neck. She was rocking us both to sleep, rocking us out of this world. I woke up once, sweating under her coat. Her body was flung away from mine, sleeping, naked.

In the morning she was crouched over me. The windows were lit up blue. She already had her clothes on. "Wake up, little mystery," she said. She put a finger to my lips. "Shh, now. We won't talk about it. Are you ready to hear my dream?"

I didn't know where I was or who I was with. I shook my head to clear it. "I dreamt you made love to me, Franny. We were off somewhere in the snow, and you made love to me."

"That's not true . . ." I started to say. If I had been

more awake I might have shot up and run from her, full of regrets and feeling monstrous. But as it was, as soon as I felt her hands on me, firmly on me, pushing me down, it was already too late to go anywhere. She kneeled by the bed and brought me to her. She took a long time. She kissed my cunt, and the inside of my thighs, and my cunt again. Her tongue slipped in and out of me, moved up and down, and in circles. Her hands moved to the small of my back and arched me up to meet her mouth, until I understood and arched myself. She gently pulled my pubic hair. She felt how wet I was and put her one wet finger to my mouth. "This is you," she said. She stroked my sides. She held me to her, and open, and for a long time my whole body moved in brilliant, widening circles. Two of her fingers pressed hard at my vagina and I screamed something as I came.

Claire was up and running to the sink. I heard her. I had my eyes closed and was moving my head from side to side on the bed. "There, little girl," she said. She held a hot, damp towel between my legs. I felt the warmth of it all the way up inside me, deeper than I'd ever felt anything before. "There's your mystery," she said. At first I thought it was a red leaf she held up in front of me. It was her hand, and there was blood all over it.

"You were a virgin."

I was sitting up, bent over, watching the towel at my crotch turn pink as I bled into it. "So this is what happens the first time?"

"To you, this is what happens."

"Not to everyone?"

"I don't know about everyone, Franny, I only know about me, and now you."

"You've never broken into anyone else's body before?"

"What a thing you are!" But she was smiling, refolding the towel to wipe the last of the blood cleanly away. My

43

thighs were red from the warmth. "See how you're blushing," she said. "Your body loves this, doesn't it?"

I got dressed and Claire made eggs and tea on the
campstove. The plows were just getting out, uncovering
the city, jarring the morning with their mirthless shaking
of chains. But between their going and coming was a silent
world that belonged neither to Thompson Street nor to
any part of any city. It was a primitive world, halfway
between sky and ground, where two women squatted before a two-burner Coleman stove the way their precursors
had squatted before a fire. We didn't gnaw bones and fling
them, though we did eat poached eggs with chopsticks, or
Claire did, while I searched the bungalow for a spoon or
fork.

"You won't find one, Franny," she said. "I don't keep
that stuff around. There aren't any drawers to look through
anyway."

"If they were scrambled, Claire, I swear I'd use my
hands, happily. But poached. I don't see how you can grab
a poached egg with those sticks. Poached don't stay still."
She was sitting cross-legged on the floor now and I sat
beside her. "Those are the eggs of the aristocracy, you
know that, don't you?"

She nodded. She was holding one whole egg up in
the air, between her thumb and forefinger. The yolk looked
alive, as if it were about to jump. Suddenly she reached
her tongue out to it and sucked the whole thing into her
mouth. She rolled her eyes up and rubbed her stomach
and fell into my lap, laughing.

"That's why I cooked them for you," she said. "I was
going to make cinnamon toast but I don't have a toaster,
or cinnamon. Isn't that aristocratic, cinnamon toast?"

"You're asking for it," I said. I rubbed her forehead,
trying to rub away the creases between her eyebrows.

"And you're touchy about it."

"No, I'm not."

"You're touchy about a lot of things you don't think you're touchy about."

"Hand me my eggs," I said.

"No. Stay with me, Franny. Tell me something. Were you so scared of me last night?"

"I've never been scared of you, Claire. I was scared you'd be scared of me."

"Why?"

"Because I don't know anything. Because I'm like a goddess to most people. I give off something, like a scent or something, that warns them away. Like I'm too good to touch. Like my body's invisible to people, and all they can see in me is my intellect."

I was caressing Claire's head, fiercely now. "Most of the time I don't even believe I really have a body, or I wasn't sure I did until this morning."

"And last night?"

"Last night in the middle of it I thought you'd leave me. You were leaving me. I saw you going off somewhere and I brought you back."

Claire sat up and held onto me, but I couldn't relax in her arms. "Okay okay okay," she said, right into my ear. "Just remember, you don't have to be a little tough guy anymore, not with sex, not with anything. I'm beginning to see you, Franny, and you're not a goddess, and you have a body. And it's a beautiful body. I love every inch of it, do you believe that?"

I did for a moment, and in that moment I opened myself to every genuine voice or action in me. As if waiting behind the door they rushed out, wetting my eyes and cheeks, and crying I thought, Ah, so this is what tears are made of.

Claire fed me a cold egg off her palm. "We're pagans," she said, "and this is pagan love."

45

Whatever she meant by that grows dimmer, not clearer when I attack it with my intellect instead of my senses. My senses tell me it wasn't just the egg, or the manner of eating it, or the sitting on the floor that made us pagans. We were uncivilized in all the good ways. I think we uncivilized each other. We always had. But especially from that morning on, we asked each other to make life interesting, to not let things be. "Never let me be guilty of an uncreative thought," was Claire's prayer, Claire's impossible dream. I was around to remind her of her dream, as she would remind me of mine, said so often some days my lips hurt with it: "Let me live on my emotions! I can sleep when I get old!"

3

Before she talked about him, I always imagined Claire's father to be a kind old anti-intellectual, part-time raiser of soybeans and a couple of goats. For his real work, I saw him as one of those saint-faced keepers of crosswalks whose raised arm and cardboard sign stop traffic for passing schoolkids. They are usually old men, full of wishes. In the warm weather they come early to work and bring lawn chairs, and sit at their corners, waiting and dreaming.

When I told Claire this she laughed. "You forget, you romantic, it's cold in Illinois, and when it's not cold it's windy, which makes a very short season for lawn chairs."

"Well, you *have* seen them dreaming," I said. "On their feet and dreaming. They all have this faraway look in their eye as if they're using that time to travel to who knows where. If you wave at them when they're off duty, waiting for the kids to come out, even the wave they wave back at you seems like it's crossing a million miles."

"I don't know about that," said Claire. "The man who kept our crosswalk used to have a black dog and he'd play fetch with it."

Her father also had a black dog, but eventually he beat it to death. While it was living, it was the only thing he and the crosswalk-keeper had in common. He was an army man, stationed in Hawaii and Alaska for what he called the best years of his life, before he met Claire's mother and let her roots take him down. He'd never been bound before, according to Claire. His travel was no daydream. It was real and compulsive, built into his character the way house and home were built into his wife's. She won, in a way. Illinois had them both for a time, for a short time. Seven years and six little Catholic kids later, and he couldn't take it anymore.

Until Claire told the story, I never believed anyone, child or parent, ever left home with only a suitcase, stealing away in the night. Not a note, not a slammed door, not even a shouted goodbye. He took two brass candlesticks that weren't worth much but were the only valuables the family had managed to acquire. He left the car, an old powder blue Valiant, and rode the bus, they supposed, or hitchhiked to who knows where. Claire was the oldest, as well as his favorite. He disappeared on her seventh birthday and in the twenty-three years since then he'd paled, in her memory, to a ghostlike smoke.

"You never heard from him at all?" I asked her. Claire and I had been lovers for less than a week, and this kind of desertion was impossible to imagine.

She shook her head. "Never. It was odd. I don't even think I liked him all that much, but I couldn't sleep nights for a long time after he was gone. At night he used to play the radio loud, Franny, the classical station. He was a big man. He scared the little kids, he was so big. He scared

48

my mother, too, I think. I remember one night he came into the room where I slept with the two babies. Everyone in the house was asleep but me and my father. The 'William Tell Overture' was going in the living room, but the whole house slept through it.

"He came in with his arms up over his head and when he got through the door he held them straight out from his shoulders like a man on a cross. I knew he was coming for me. I didn't know why. I wanted whatever it was over with quickly, so I sat up to meet him. He hadn't expected that. My face almost touched his own leaning over. He smelled of mothballs, which is still what I think of whenever I smell whiskey."

"God, Claire. What was it? What did he want?"

"He said he wanted to dance."

"He *what*?"

"He said, 'Honey, up and come dance with me.' His voice was crackly, not a whisper. It woke the other kids out of their dreams, and they yelled, and Mother came running."

"And what did he do?"

"He just stood there. He backed up to the doorway and stood there. He watched Mother comforting and tucking in, tucking me in, too, although I was five or six then and too old for that. She kept asking me if I was all right, and putting her hands on my face, while my father just watched it all like he was the door itself standing open. Later I heard them get into it in the living room, but the fights never kept me awake, just the music."

"Claire?"

"Mmm?"

"That's not dancing music, the 'William Tell Overture.' "

"I've thought of that," she said.

The only other thing she told me about him was that she felt free of him now. That he had gone from solid to liquid to gas in her life, and as far as she was concerned he was hanging up around the stars somewhere, where the crosswalk-keepers traveled only in their dreams. She was interested in my father, though, from the first she heard of him.

"He's literary," I told her. "He knows things like the first few pages of *Waiting for Godot.*"

"What do you mean he knows them?"

"He's memorized them. He'll start off, 'A country road. A tree. Evening. Estragon says: Nothing to be done.' "

"But Franny, that's nuts. What does he get from it?"

"It fills the night, I guess. He doesn't sleep much, so he'll stay up learning lines. I think it's a comfort to him that there's great art in the world—great art and great recipes for chicken. Chicken done a thousand ways, the same thought or idea expressed differently by different artists. Those things make him happy, I can't explain it. He eats what he cooks, and he memorizes what he reads. It gives him a life, Claire, that's all I can say."

Of course I could have said more, but I decided to let Claire see for herself. We took the train to Mine Brook, and Claire was like a little puppy, jumping up, roaming from window to window as if she were afraid to miss something. I realized I'd never seen her out of the city before, though northeastern New Jersey is still, in some ways, New York. But when the tenements and gray skylines of cemeteries gave way to pink tract homes and hedges, some light came on in her. She leaned between the seats and sent her eyes outside to gather the rushing landscape to her.

It was an awkward landscape that day, the first day of spring on the calendar but nothing to show for it in the earth itself. It was, and we were, between seasons: soggy patches of snow in fenced yards, trees unbudded. And earlier, on the outskirts of the city, none of T. S. Eliot's lonely men in shirtsleeves, leaning out of windows, the hearty who bear almost any weather, any off-season, to smoke their pipes in peace. There was only the laundry hanging out above the train tracks, which made Claire laugh. "It must just get dirty all over again," she said, "out in air like this." For my benefit she had quit cigarettes that week, and the sheets and shirts and underwear hanging up bravely in all that smog and soot, reminded her of her own lungs.

I say we were between seasons because the weekend before I had let this woman make love to me, and since then we had met only once, over coffee, in the neutral setting of our favorite Hamburger Heaven. I had made the date and she'd kept it, though she'd been late. She came in, opening her coat with one hand and lifting and tousling her hair with the other. The restaurant was crowded and I watched her looking for me. I watched to see what others saw when they saw her, but all I saw was a woman whose face and hair and body appeared, in the window glare, to be on fire.

She sat down.

"I've needed to see you, Claire."

I'd already ordered her coffee and it had cooled, and she didn't take it onto her spoon and blow on it the way she usually did, but gulped it. "I've needed to see you too," she said, but neither of us was convinced.

I let her talk about her work, which she complained had been keeping her from me. A new bunch of Brancusi heads had arrived and she'd been up day and night at the museum, preparing the exhibit. "It's harder than it sounds, Franny. The trick is to arrange them so they don't look like they're talking to each other, but you don't want them turning away from each other either." I think this was our first conversation of avoidance.

She had gone her way and I mine, but the next few days had a weight and dullness to them I couldn't shake off. By the time the weekend came I'd decided not to try to define us or even pluralize the Franny and Claire. She had reason to be wary of the *we*, I told myself. Anyone did. It was so often used to reduce a relationship rather than to expand it.

But the truth was that I was just beginning to know what a skittish creature Claire was under her skin. The afternoon after the morning she made love to me, I had stayed to help her pull a large paper-mache teapot over her head. In this costume, and wearing a sandwich board, she walked the 53rd Street block between Madison and Fifth Avenue, advertising the Palladium Coffee Shop for three dollars an hour. This was what Claire called creative moonlighting—creative and essential. A few hours of this on occasional weekends kept her in coffee and ham salad sandwiches, and besides that she seemed to truly love the work. She dressed at home and rode the subway uptown, navigating through two eyeholes under her spout. The spout was removable so it wouldn't get crushed, and she carried it under one arm, the sandwich board under the other. The costume had sleeves sticking out the sides of the pot, like the ridiculously undersized wings of a cartoon bird. I was helping my friend struggle into these as she described her route to me, the stationery store and beauty shop, and the deli with hams hanging in its window.

"They're plastic hams, Franny." Her voice came clearly through the chicken wire and paper-mache, though I couldn't see her. I could only see her legs in brown tights sticking out the bottom of the pot. "They're the most luscious pink and purple hams you can imagine, though not quite heavy enough to be real."

I didn't need to ask whether or not it ever got monotonous, this journey from lamppost to lamppost, meter to meter, out and back along the same small orbit two or three times an hour, because obviously to Claire it didn't. "Oh, it's never the same," she said. "The earth turns every time you take a step. The cars at the light change; the light changes. Even the buildings move. And that's just what my eyes can see. If I could hear through this damn thing, that would add another world to the world. Besides that, what climbs into this teapot is never the same."

What had climbed into the teapot that day? I wanted to know, and decided to find out. I took her hand. She was almost too wide for the stairs. Slowly we made our way down to the snowy street, down to the subway where the train came too soon. I stood on the platform, tempted to blow a kiss to a teapot behind the window, aware of how often we let those graffitied walls and noisy tin wheels carry us from each other. My face showed all this, I'm sure, and possibly Claire's did too, though she was tucked safely inside her costume and all I had of her wasn't her but a couple of empty eyeholes. A short Mediterranean man standing at the front of the car looked her up and down in a way that boiled me.

I had decided to follow her. I caught the next train and surfaced at 53rd Street in time to see her half a block ahead of me, struggling into her sandwich board. She was struggling just to stay afloat where the snow hadn't yet been shoveled. I longed to give up my place in the anonymous crowd and rush up and let her lean on me, but she rolled across the street and down the next block. In front of the Palladium she stopped to put on her spout. She bent forward to study herself in the glass. She arranged the spout's angle, readjusted the pot and sandwich board, then began her slow, rocking walk east. The rock had been Claire's invention, a detail she loved. It was supposed to bring to mind a boiling kettle.

Most of that chilly afternoon I sat on a fire hydrant, hidden from her, and watched her. In the cold, her breath came out the spout in little white puffs which made her costume more authentic. Once I came up close behind her, as close as I dared without jostling her chicken wire, and I thought I could hear her singing or humming inside.

Dear friend. I tried to see her life that day the way she might: that long narrow look ahead of her through the eyeholes that allowed her to meditate as she walked. She didn't count the pausing or passing strangers as I did. To the bundled child or two who ploughed off-course to tug on her chicken wire or shriek baby talk at her knees, she was oblivious. And she couldn't have noticed the pug in boots and a little knit coat that stopped to sniff and lift a leg on hers. She was numb, poor Claire, but not just her legs that surely shook in their little thin tights as the late afternoon cold came down on us. She was numb to the rush and flow of people around her, though she'd taken in every detail of those plastic hams.

My friend had said something earlier that day and as I watched her it came to me again. She had been down on her knees, looking up into the cave of the teapot I was generously lowering over her head. "Franny," she had said, "this may be my life's work, you know, just getting myself out of this costume." There had been an echo around her waist as her head and shoulders disappeared inside.

I had understood the words then only in the simple way because that was all my hearing had been good for, but from my fire hydrant it occurred to me that she did feel trapped by her way of seeing the world as separate from herself; that her teapot was her solitude, a sort of high loneliness that she told herself she needed and loved, and out of this she might well become the best at it of anyone I would ever meet.

I had watched her combing her hair one afternoon in the bungalow when she thought I was asleep. She stood in front of the tall windows with her back to me. The sun cut her in half so she seemed like an upper body floating in the darkness of the room. Her hair was flipped back behind her shoulders and the comb easily cut through it. There was nothing to untangle. It was only out of the pleasure in the motion that she combed it at all. One hand

54

rose and fell with the comb and the other hand followed, just to feel the smoothness and softness of her own hair. She arched her back and shook out her head. She put the comb in her mouth and set her fingers in her part, following it back from her forehead. From her neck she ran her hands upward across her scalp, pushing the hair forward, then combing it down again. I had the shivers watching her. I felt like it was my first intimate moment with her or with anyone. She was so private and distant even then, combing in her own world. She would have blushed to know I was awake and taking her in.

That was the first time I saw her give in to herself. The second was when we made love. But though I sat in my seat on the Erie Lackawanna and reassured myself with memories of my friend's narrow bed, and the recent sweetness and closeness of our company, I couldn't shake the vision of Claire disappearing inside her teapot from below as I held it, and the knowledge that I hadn't touched or really even talked to her since then. All week that vision had returned like a fine netting through which I had to see and remember, dividing sweetness and Franny and Claire into tiny uncountable squares. Like a look through a microscope that showed the most exquisite leaf or lichen in all its ordinary and irreconcilable parts. And each time, in my memory, the teapot with Claire inside grew larger, and I smaller. Now as I watched my friend hop the aisle to settle in one smooth cane seat after another, unable to find any real resting place on that train, I hardly knew who I was watching.

But she was happy that day and her happiness was contagious. I caught it. Even the conductor caught it, thinking Claire much younger than she was and stopping in his passage to point out the hotels and hardware stores of every town bisected by the track. We were moving slowly but surely into a more rural New Jersey. Broad towns that lumbered after the train for a mile past the station, then gave up into fields of would-be green. Names like Short Hills, Berkeley Heights and Basking Ridge. Conflicting hints of romance and snobbery that made it both possible and difficult for me to admit I lived here in the most misunderstood state in the country.

It was more my parents' home now than my own. If I lived anywhere it was on this train, commuting in and out of the city to sell hamsters all day at my father's pet shop. This was only one of his business ventures. He also owned a diner in Brooklyn, a wicker furniture store and two small bakeries on the Lower East Side. Years ago, just out of college, he'd sold Bowie knives out of a room not much larger than a foot locker. Then rare books. Then stamps. Then finally, oddly, antique gum dispensers. All of this was barely a living for a bachelor, even with simple tastes, so my father taught himself to play the stock market, and investing what little extra he had, got lucky and won.

He wasn't new wealth, exactly, although he'd never in his life asked for any help from the old wealth he was related to. His father was a sort of dandy, who terrified him; frivolous in all ways, a Gatsby without Gatsby's spine. He traveled abroad, he went through wives—my father's mother and at least two after that. He threw parties and ran with a crowd he didn't belong in. His money couldn't keep up with him, although it never entirely ran out. He offered my father the Ivy League college of his choice. The country was at war. My father accepted. I think he suffered some small guilt about this, both filial and patriotic, though there was nothing imaginary about the poor eyesight that kept him from being drafted.

My mother's family ran a small motor repair business down in SoHo, a few doors away from where Claire's apartment building stood. It was a failing enterprise, and always had been, until 1945 when a couple of well-timed events turned their luck around. First, Emanuel Simmons advertised his custom electric wheelchair, and second, the war ended and hundreds of legless vets came home to a future confined to just such a contraption. After some quick thinking and quick talking, my grandparents moved themselves into position as the only power chair repair specialists in the country. The business took off. My mother wore real silk stockings for the first time and rouged her cheeks, and darkened her eyes with store-bought makeup instead of a stub of charcoal. In 1950, window shopping, I like to think, for a leatherbound *Gulliver's Travels,* or whatever might have been her own equivalent to *The Sketchbooks of Botticelli,* she met my father. He was twenty-six, she had just turned thirty. They were married, and two years later I was born.

Until I was seventeen we lived in the city and spent summers in one beach cottage or another along the Massachusetts shore. I went to good, private schools that still believed in the separation of the sexes. My friends were the daughters of celebrities; except in the summers, there were no sons in my life until college. But my main company, by choice, was always my parents, and especially my father. One reason for this was because my mother worked, and when she wasn't working, in summer she was sitting on the beach. My father worked at home, caretaking his investments from a small bedroom-turned-office.

He was still playing the stock market, though no longer consistently winning. Those numbers seemed to matter less to him now that he was launched, and his wife and child with him. The small businesses mattered more, and he did well with them. Together we went around to see them every weekend. We employed ourselves, boxing eclairs in the bakery or scooping guppies in the pet shop. My father was beginning to be an excellent cook, and on any Sunday morning at the diner he'd do an eggs benedict all-you-can-eat for a dollar. Roger, the regular short-order cook, would lend him his high, white chef's hat and a clean apron, and lean under the exhaust fan telling unfunny jokes through the gaps between his teeth. He was mostly gaps, my father pointed out, and his laugh came like the *sss-sss-sss* of frying bacon.

The diner clientele were steady, dough-faced Brooklynites who chewed in an exaggerated way and sprayed food everywhere when they argued. In some ways they were the opposite of my father, and I realize now that's why he took refuge there. They loved him. They called him King Gustav the Great. "We like eating in places where the owner has strength of character," they all told him. They used the Yiddish, *mensch*. They praised him in Russian and Polish. Besides school French, this was my earliest experience of foreign languages, and standing beside my father those Sundays at the diner, I had my first taste of leaving home.

I think from the beginning he had me in mind for the pet shop. When I was younger I loved the fake wilderness of it. The birds were my favorite, then the fish. There were a couple of clownish monkeys I liked, and a male raccoon the size of a wedding cake. But besides that, the kittens and puppies bored me, and I grew to hate the hamsters—a simple case of overexposure. By the time I met Claire I had managed that pet shop for two years, and hamsters were the only inventory you could count on getting rid of.

"They're like the junk food of pets," I complained to her one day.

"Don't be cruel," she told me. "Who knows what they're saying about you."

When my parents moved to the country, I supposedly moved with them, and for the most part I liked it out there where I could find the stars. But I wasn't as ready as they were for early retirement, and besides that I went to college and worked in the city five days a week so sometimes it was easier to stay in their little apartment than to commute home. After I met Claire, I seldom saw my parents anymore, even on weekends. Oddly enough, it was she, not

I, who wondered aloud, a few minutes out of Mine Brook: "They'll want to know who the new man in your life is, Franny, and what will you tell them?"

The green convertible wasn't there, which meant my mother had again forgotten. Or was late. Or Britta hadn't passed on my message of two days before: *Arriving Saturday, 11:22, at Mine Brook. Friend with me. No need to break out the band.* This last was in reference to a time two years before when I'd come home from a semester in Rome and my father had gathered all his musical friends together on the back of a hay wagon—two trumpets, violins, even a bass drum—and this impromptu orchestra had met me at the station.

"Where was your mother in all that?" Claire asked when I told her the story.

"In New York, finishing up business, I guess. She was always busy the first few years after they moved out here. She jumped on any excuse to take a trip to the city. She was a buyer, actually a fashion designer turned buyer, and buyers are like that. They have to be mobile, either upwardly or—"

"Or in circles."

"Yeah. That still seems to be her favorite direction."

If I painted an unfavorable picture of my mother that day, it was at least no surprise to Claire; after all, she had known me since December. And I'm sure, setting foot on the platform of the station, she sensed something about my parents' marriage that has taken me the years since then to discover: That however stable it was, it was also tedious and unhappy. That was its stability. Their personalities never met, could never meet. If they had, it would have been in explosion rather than in harmony.

What might she have seen, getting off the train, to tell her this? A single yellow cab waiting for a passenger (but we are the only passengers). An errant boy and girl, adolescents giggling hopelessly at their inability to caress each other well in public. Sharing a bench with them, Liza, the town mumbler, bent over, staring at her shoes. They're next-to-new men's wing tips, something my own father would have worn years before (and perhaps these are his, discarded, that she's rescued from the Goodwill bin). Everything in sight—this occurs to me now, not then—is a kind of amateur version of its New York City equivalent. The boy and girl are laughing, when theirs should be serious blundering. The cab is sitting with its engine off, not pursuing a fare; the driver asleep over a newspaper, not leaning on his horn. And Liza—even a name like that, not down and out enough, almost royalty—with those ridiculous but too new shoes, and no paper sack with bottle, no bulky shopping bag. Just what her pockets can hold, that's all she walks off with. And whatever it is she's mumbling never gets past her lips as sound.

What Claire stepped down into that morning was exactly what my mother hated and my father loved with all his heart. The harmless. The quaint. The unprofessional. The backstage world of understudies and stagehands who never get their time under the lights and are glad of it. A sleepy, slow-moving world where meeting the train may be a day's work, so arriving two hours ahead of time is not unheard of. My father, I see, lived in the space between events, my mother in the events themselves. New Jersey was his choice, not hers, for that reason, and after a marriage of having it her way, I don't know why she gave in to him for these last years of their lives.

Obviously, meeting Claire and me at the station wasn't much of an event in my mother's world, otherwise she would have been there.

"Look for a green MG convertible," I said. Claire and I sat on the curb next to the taxi, shading our eyes against the sun.

"What? Your mother drives a sports car, Franny? You've got to be kidding."

"It's her station car. It's an old wreck she just drives around town."

"And your father? Why couldn't he be the one to meet us?"

"He doesn't have a license," I said. "His eyes are shot with all the reading he does, and he's got cataracts. He's terrified of the operation, so it's possible in a few years he'll be legally blind."

This surprised Claire, as if she'd already drawn a character for my father and I was contradicting it. "What a shame," she said. "Losing the part of himself he most loves. Like Jake what's-his-name in *The Sun Also Rises*."

"Not exactly," I smiled.

"Somehow I can't picture him feeling his way around the kitchen. He manages?"

I nodded. "Well, there's Britta. But there's always been Britta."

"Who's that?"

"A beloved ghoul."

"Seriously."

"The help," I said. "Our hired hand. She's a beachball who rolled in years ago and never rolled out. She's a tiny, round German woman who's been with us for years, ever since I can remember. She cooks and cleans and lives with us in the winters, and every other summer she goes back to Germany. She taught my father to cook. He adores her, even though they used to fight over the kitchen."

"And now?"

"And now she's too ancient to do much. She bakes, squeezes the orange juice. Mostly she sits in the sun with her feet up and listens to opera."

"Opera!"

"I came into the kitchen once and she and Gus—"

"Who's Gus?"

"My father. They were rolling out biscuits and singing along with *La Traviata,* putting their doughy hands to their foreheads and the whole bit. Britta was sobbing. It was near the end. She was standing on a little stool to reach the table better, but the stool was wobbling. It was swaying back and forth and my father caught her as she went over, right where in the opera the tubercular woman falls against the pillows and dies."

"What then?"

"Nothing. The opera ended and later we ate the biscuits."

It sounded so simple. I wonder if my friend knew then what occurred to me only much later, months later when Claire was overseas and I had come to see my family in a more sympathetic light: That Britta was a wedge between my parents, just as the move to the country was and I was too. Whatever they once shared they now used to keep themselves apart. I saw it as stinginess. Claire called it the unbinding of souls.

We waited half an hour then knocked on the windshield of the taxi to wake the driver. "I'm the laziest man in the world," he warned us, "but I can whistle." Neither my friend nor I knew what to do with this information.

"He's got a square head," Claire whispered. We were throwing my pack in the trunk.

"He lives here," I whispered back.

The cab smelled of the bottom of shoes, mixed with the adhesive tape the driver had used to bandage his seats. Claire stuck her face out the window all up and down the not-yet-green hills, and past the turned fields of fox-hunting country. She waved to a couple of tractors wearing blue ribbons of smoke. They were disking, and the earth opened up behind the disks in a dark brown wake. I remembered farming was in her blood, and this was spring, and something primordial might be going on in her too deep for me to see.

"We're close, Claire."

"What?" She brought her head in.

"We're almost home."

What passed on both sides of us were small farm operations, owned by the wealthy who raised hay for their jumpers and thoroughbreds. My parents' place, coming up on the left, was one of the few properties that couldn't be called an estate. The house was a square, white clapboard chunk, larger than it needed to be on the outside, but on the inside, compared to the way they'd lived in the city, nothing fancy. It was my father's influence this time, where before it had been my mother's. Around the house was a small island of lawn, and out back my father's garden. There was no driveway to speak of, just a short length of asphalt reaching off the main road. Claire had her hand out the window, cupping the onrushing wind, and I'll never forget what she said to me before the taxi slowed to turn our corner: "Try it, Franny. It feels like a woman's breast coming at you."

I paid the driver and the cab took off.

"I've wanted to kiss you for miles," I told my friend. I was looking at the face of the house as if it were something to be shot rather than lived in.

"Well, kiss me then," she said. And then, "What's that?"

I hadn't heard a thing. "What's what?"

"That. It sounds like somebody saying a mantra."

It started as a low-pitched murmur that got clearer as it came closer. It was a man's voice, and the man sounded like he was coming around the side of the house. He was saying, "Mad dog, mad dog," over and over again, moving toward us though still out of sight.

What we finally saw when we saw him was a white-headed figure—his hair had all turned at once, in a matter

63

of months, when he was forty—wearing light blue pajamas and a green plaid bathrobe. He had on a pair of white hightop basketball sneakers, unlaced, and he was leaning forward, looking for something on the ground. He didn't see us. He kicked the bushes several times and straightened up, as if expecting something to fly out the top of them. As he came closer, we could see the way his black-rimmed glasses almost took over his face. In his body he looked like me, though not so thin, but with the same habit of making himself seem bigger by letting his limbs hang loosely as he walked, as if he were feeding himself to the air around him.

"Your father?" asked Claire.

I nodded. By then he had reached the front of the house and the *mad dog*'s were louder and more urgent. "He's lost his cat," I said. "Gone out in the midday sun. She's a beauty we found curled up on the hood of his car outside the Brooklyn diner years ago."

So this was Claire's introduction to Gus, though the actual shaking of hands—his awkward formality, not hers—didn't come until several minutes later, inside the door of my parents' home, with the door neither fully open nor shut. He hugged and kissed me first, then held me away while he took in Claire. For a few moments he seemed shy of her, almost afraid of her. At the time I understood it simply as the surprise that we'd arrived.

"My god, Fru, who ruined you?" He ruffled my hair, laughing. "It looks like a dog bit it."

"Which is just what I don't need to hear," I said, suddenly realizing that Gus had given me every haircut of my life, until this one.

He gave Claire the tour, taking her first to the kitchen where a young girl I'd never laid eyes on before stood in front of the sink drying the breakfast dishes. I say young. She was at least eighteen or nineteen, and possibly older than me. After meeting Claire, I no longer trusted my ability to guess a woman's age. She was beautiful, in all the ways Claire and I were not. Hers ran along the lines of a classic beauty, with creamy skin, high cheeks, dark hair and eyes. What struck me, even from across the kitchen, was how long her eyelashes were. They were genuine, as was everything else about her. She didn't use makeup. Makeup didn't look like it was even part of her vocabulary. She was wearing a very plain white uniform, like a nurse's uniform, short-sleeved and baggy enough to be Britta's. A perfectly timed opening in the clouds dropped a bar of sunlight across her as the three of us came into the kitchen.

She was Jenny, very Scottish, and standing in for Britta for the week. Gus introduced us, turning a slow circle that meant to include all three women in the room.

"What's the matter with Britta?" I asked.

"Kidney stones. They think. Your mother took her in to the doctor this morning, and then to her sister's." Britta's sister was a nun who had a wide, boat face and lived in the Bronx. "Your two trains passed."

"I didn't see the car," I said.

"It's in the shop for a few hours," said Gus, "having its tonsils out."

Done with the dishes now and unsure where next to put her hands, Jenny was awesomely polite, as well as lovely. This was the first time my eyes had looked at a woman this way, immediately taking in the physical and letting that propel me. After all, Claire and I had spent months preparing our minds for our bodies. As we stood there, I half expected the clouds to close up again, taking this woman with them. I know she wouldn't have minded, shy as she was.

This scene was what Claire would call a clear manifestation of the dream—Gus's dream. *Man with Three Wives* might have been the name of the painting of us; everything alternately washed in sun, then not, and our awkwardness perfectly reflected in the changing light. Gus felt responsible for the conversation, though that was always my mother's art, not his, and at least one of the two strangers in the room saw right through him until he was equal to the white wall behind him. I can't speak for Jenny, but Claire, I know, noticed what was written out and framed on that wall, and at that moment in time she might have questioned the purity of motive of the hand, my father's, that hung it there. It was a Ramayana quote: *I have witnessed in this jungle graceful creatures passing fair.* Was he, Gus, for us or against us? she might have wondered. How witnessed? and through whose eyes a jungle?

Out of this dream, or in the middle of it, Gus had her by the arm and was leading her to the tomatoes—little four-inch plants held up by dental floss and popsicle sticks, growing out of egg cartons on the windowsill. He pointed at his peas, already coming up out of the thin snow on this side of the garden.

"Franny remembers the locusts," I heard him say. "Don't you, Fru? You were a baby and they came and stuck to your hair."

"I don't remember anything before kindergarten," I said, "but I thought I didn't have any hair. Wasn't I an ugly baby?"

"You were chubby and almost bald, that's true, but not ugly."

Jenny whispered, "There's no such thing as an ugly baby."

"Not true," said Claire. "I was an ugly baby."

"Oh, you weren't," said Gus.

"I was a blue baby. I almost suffocated to death. I was premature and blue, and on top of that I caught jaundice and turned green."

Jenny's laugh sounded more like a little cough. "Oh, excuse me," she said. "I just thought it was a bit funny."

"It *was* a bit funny," said Claire. She was looking at

Jenny the way she sometimes looked at me, when she wanted to say, "Stop acting spineless. It doesn't suit you."

"Fru had a heart murmur," Gus said. "Instead of lub dub, lub dub, the sound in her chest was lub dub shh, lub dub shh."

"As if someone in there were dragging their feet," said Claire.

"They still are," I said, though I knew it wasn't true. She was the only one who heard me, and she smiled at the corner of her mouth.

Gus was on to other things. In our apartment in the city he had filled his study with books—rare books, leather-bound, paperback and used books. Everything from the *Bhagavad Gita* and Homer, to Karl Marx and Aldous Huxley. Emily Dickinson was a favorite of his, as was Virginia Woolf, and added to these a couple of fly-by-nights, Ian Fleming and Agatha Christie, whom he used as a kind of sweet rest from the exacting work of ploughing through so much magnificent writing. The spy stories and mysteries were like dessert to him, no substitute for the entree. He thought like this, of books in terms of food. It was natural; they were the twin passions of his life.

Where my parents now lived they had about half the space they'd had in the apartment. The house's great white façade was just that, a misrepresentation of what went on inside. My parents' bedroom was upstairs (twin beds, flannel sheets in the winter), and mine was on the first floor, underneath theirs. My mother had a study of sorts, the old laundry room with the hot and cold faucets still protruding from the wall above her desk. As a result of this they sent the laundry out now, and it always amused me how easily they'd arrived at this convention of the wealthy out of an odd lack of choice about the whole thing. Or it was a choice my mother had made years ago: To be a businesswoman, not a housewife.

Gus, however, had no place to park his books, except in the room he took on as his own sort of study—the kitchen. He'd simply filled the cupboards with them, and weeded out the boxes of glass and chinaware so all that was left could fit around the books. Often, as he stirred or chopped, he'd have Mark Twain or Joyce Cary open in front of him, as if absorbing their recipe for a humorous stew.

"This is a wonderful one," he told Claire, reaching up over her head for *The Horse's Mouth*. But she was an inch or two taller than him and already had her hand on it. She brought it down herself.

"I know," she said. "Art and artists. That book brought me through a winter of deep depression once. Listen to this, Franny." She turned to me. I hadn't known about that deep depression. She read: " 'Coker'—that's the barkeep—'thought a bit with her nose out of the door. Like a tit looking through a fence.' "

"That's got to be the English," said Jenny in a small voice she wanted no one to hear.

"That's what?" said Claire.

"I said it's English, the author is. It's English humor. Only the English would put a . . . oh, I don't know." She reddened. "It just strikes me as English."

"The tit through the fence is what does it," said Claire. Jenny cringed. "That's what's English."

At that three-letter word I saw Gus's shoulders jump. I couldn't see his face. I was standing behind him, closer to the sink and Jenny. He had never been a prude, or even proper enough, really, for the company my mother brought home, or dragged him into, but he was unaccustomed to this kind of explicitness, if you could call it that. I, for one, had never challenged him in that way at all. Still, language was language, and he had often told me how he loved every word of it. So it wasn't so much the utterance of "tit" that sent his shoulders flying up, as the matter-of-fact way she uttered it. I was the only one who guessed what had really moved Claire, and it was the opposite of matter-of-fact. It was her unwillingness not to provoke when she thought provocation would bring all involved out of some sort of lie and nearer to an honesty.

At that moment in the kitchen, what she was rebelling against, I believe, was to be thought of by my father as one of Ramayana's graceful creatures passing fair. She knew, as well as all women at least intuitively do, that she was just such a creature—understood by Ramayana, but possibly not by a man like my father. She didn't know Gus, but she didn't take him on faith the way everyone else did; the way I did, and always had. I think she was talking to me every time she responded to him. She wanted to push him. She wanted to see what he was made of. She might have been jealous of him, or she just might have needed to know whether he was worth all the love, conscious and unconscious, that I gave him. If she wanted it for herself instead, so be it. She felt my loyalty divided, and she couldn't really love me until it wasn't.

Jenny fled politely to tidy other things in other rooms. I could have stayed around to show my intellectual bones ("Franny can tell us all about Machiavelli, can't you, Fru?") but I was plagued by my voices. I left those two in the kitchen, wishing my father a less ratty pair of pajamas and at least a pair of socks. It was his custom to stay unkempt until noon, but it was after that now and the coach had turned back to a pumpkin. All his seams were showing, suddenly, all his soft spots. To my retreating eye Claire seemed the parent now and Gus the little boy, which made me, for the first time, his equal.

"Going, Fran?" he asked.

"Yes."

"The jack-in-the-pulpits are out."

"By the swamp?"

"There, and back farther by the broken fence. You remember?"

"Do you want me to come with you?" asked Claire.

"No. I'll go alone. I'll take you down there tomorrow."

And they *were* out, in bunches of three and four, brave souls; the only company for crocuses at that time of year. The little green and purple pulpit, not yet unfurled, and hiding inside it the pale green jack. I could find him only if I knelt and lifted the top flap of the flower. I soaked my knees this way. My feet were already wet. But the chill took away some of the noise in my head and the kneeling gave me the ground. It was a ground I loved, after all, even in this awkward season. The fiddleheads would be out in no time, and the frail gray buds of horsechestnut and hickory. Then everything green; a greener green in August, almost half a year from now. A month more and the nuts would be all over these woods, the leaves a light cracking underfoot.

When I came home a thin steam was rising from the hood of the MG. Katheryn had just arrived. I caught sight of her in the doorway, her calf-length, camel hair coat open with the belt hanging. She was leaning over a terrier.

"Oh Frances, it's you," said my mother, glancing up from the dog at her feet. Her eyes looked exhausted. "Rapunzel's carried in a woodchuck."

Rapunzel was my mother's prize Dandie Dinmont, a stumpy-legged, salt-and-pepper colored creature, eager to attack anything that crossed paths with her including a human leg. Including her own sons, Marcus and Julius, who lived with us as well. They had inherited the same fighting instinct, so the three were in constant battle. The only time I had seen them united was in their hunting sprees, when three abreast they would cross the fields, noses deep in the stubble, zigging and zagging in beautiful formation until they had found and surrounded a wood-chuck hole. The woodchucks didn't stand a chance.

But apparently Rapunzel had killed this one herself. Barkus and Drool, as I had nicknamed her offspring, were nowhere in sight. She lay on her back in what I called asking-for-it position. Her tongue was out, blood was matted in her hair, and between us, like a doormat on the top step, lay the plump brown body of the loser.

"Why, Rap," I said, "Rapacious. I didn't know you had it in you, you old girl. You old blind thing." The hair was worn thin around her nipples which stood up like black warts across her belly.

Katheryn was cooing softly, "Oh my baby, what a sight you are. Frances, help me dear. Her ears are absolutely chewed."

I brought a bowl of peroxide and warm water from the downstairs bathroom, and Rapunzel's towel and blanket. Gus and Claire had gone walking was all Jenny could tell me, though she did prove helpful in another area. It turned out the cooking and cleaning were only part-time, and the nurse's uniform was for real.

I watched them. At first it was Katheryn who swabbed and Jenny who held those kicking terrier feet. But my mother, for all her good intentions, had always been hopelessly squeamish and only half brave enough to cover it up. Jenny recognized stubbornness, and she knew the art of imperceptible movement. It wasn't long before she had all the doctoring in her hands, and my mother was the one with her arms wrapped around Rapunzel, talking, talking to the walls, to the dog, even to the dead woodchuck. "The size of that wretched animal! Come out to find his shadow, and huff! there you were, lucky darling. Lucky, lucky not to have been swept down his hole!"

It was curious the way my mother warmed to certain strangers, while she had no clue in the world how to em-

71

brace a daughter. Jenny was perfect for her, obsequious and shy. She was also on the payroll and I wasn't. So I waited, as I often waited, through the Scottish origins of Dandie Dinmonts, through this nursing school and that: Katheryn's questions, Jenny's answers. By my mother's standards it was a successful interaction. The space was filled. Silence was sent back underground, back to that now empty woodchuck hole perhaps, which had been the source of all this talk.

The dog had been kissed and let outside again before Katheryn really looked at me for the first time. "My goodness, Frances, you've absolutely butchered your hair!" she said. "Too *bad* you never saw her before this, Jenny. Oh Fran, why? She had beautiful hair; you really did, dear. Long and blonde. Like a goddess."

"I'm not blonde, Mother."

"Yes, you used to be. You were my little towhead." She reached out to touch my hair, then brought her hand back, embarrassed.

"It won't bite you, Katheryn."

"I'm *sick* about this. I could see if it were terribly in fashion, but it's just not a fashion cut."

"I like it," I said, meaning I liked the idea of it, though Claire herself admitted I'd be better off next time going to a barber.

"Oh you *can't* like it, Fran. It's horrid. It makes a little boy out of you again."

The "again" meant that I'd grown up with my father's knives instead of dolls, and put pants on over my dresses. "Do you like it, Jenny?" I asked. Luckily the door opened at that moment and Claire came in, followed by a twilight so gray and cold I shivered to try and throw it off me.

"I found this on the step," she said, to my mother more than anyone. Across her open palms rested the woodchuck.

"Get that *out* of here," said Katheryn. "That belongs

outside. Take it to the woods, Frances. Show her where the woods are so she can take it."

"Toss it outside," I said. "We'll get rid. of it later. Katheryn hates those things. They tear up her dogs."

Claire shrugged. "Looks like this one didn't." She turned and lobbed it toward the hedge, faint streak of the athlete in her throw. "Dogs one, critters zero," she said. She looked terribly unhappy in that moment, with the dark sky rising out of her shoulder. I heard the kitchen door open and close, and Gus in there whistling, shaking off his galoshes.

Katheryn said, "Introduce us, Frances."

"Maybe I should go out and come in again," said Claire.

Though she hadn't moved, I grabbed her arm to keep her in the room, to keep myself in the room. What was it in her that calmed me? Her elbow calmed me as I held it.

There was no shaking of hands. Katheryn had finally taken off her coat and now she held it tightly in front of her. She was taller than my father, and just slightly taller than Claire. She was slender, dressy, a graying redhead. She'd had her hair poofed that morning and it was still stiff. It clung to her head like a helmet.

She wore her face like a mask, but a tasteful one. She used only what she called "crucial" makeup—wrinkle destroyers and smoothers of the hard edge. She was fifty-six and my father fifty-two, but for having lived in and looked out at the same world for so long, I had never seen two faces so unequally worn. The lines had just never settled on Gus, perhaps because he no longer saw most of what he looked out at. But Katheryn, Katheryn's eyes had always been too big, and as if to make room for them her skin had buckled.

Claire made sense of it this way. "Look, Franny, how many years of poverty did that woman endure before she came into her money?"

73

"Oh god, Claire. Longer than I've lived. She was close to thirty."

"Well, that's it then. That's where the worry lines come from. Listen. This is what I think. I think you get your face the same way you get your teeth. The baby face goes, and in comes the one you're stuck with for the rest of your life."

"That's crazy."

"No. I mean it. That's not to say you don't look different at seventeen than you will at seventy, but all the makings are there. What's written is written, and every year just takes away a little more of the fluff that hides the writing. Your mother's been uncovered, Franny, and Gus too; but whoever or whatever wrote her childhood wrote very hard and very dark, and that's what you're seeing now."

"You should have let us know, darling," said Katheryn. "You should have told someone—Britta—anyone, you were coming."

"I called Britta."

"Well, she never said a word about it."

Jenny excused herself, carrying off the bowl and bloody towel. It was this about her, Claire told me later, this constant walking on and walking off that reminded her of Alfred Hitchcock.

"Does Austin know you're here?"

"Mother, we've been here all afternoon."

"Who's Austin?" asked Claire.

"My father," I said.

"What's Gus then?"

"That's the nickname they gave him in prep school."

"Gus? Is it short for something?"

I shrugged. "I don't know."

"It's short for Gusto," said my mother with a hard, quick laugh. "Do you girls know where you're sleeping?"

"Claire and I will just take my room."

My friend flushed. I was happy to see it. Katheryn stopped in the middle of hanging up her coat. "Oh, I don't think that's so smart," she said. "You just won't be comfortable."

"We'll be fine," I said.

"You won't be fine."

"I'll gladly sleep on the floor somewhere," said Claire.

"Oh, you *can't* sleep on the floor."

"Let her sleep on the floor," I said. "She likes it. Her bed's as hard as the floor anyway."

When two people are guarding something from a third, every word between them is a potential bomb. "Bed" was like this. I heard myself say it and I saw Claire flinch at the same time. How it landed on Katheryn I'll never know. She was immersed in the closet and only came out saying, "We have a nice cot somewhere. If Frances can find it I'm sure she'll help you set it up." For a second she seemed disoriented. "I'm sorry. It's Elaine, isn't it?"

"No, Claire," I said.

"Oh, Claire," she laughed. "Like Claire de Lune."

We still called it supper at my house, though every neighbor for miles said dinner. That afternoon Gus had put together a chicken *molé,* and now he brought it out steaming in its dark juices like a miniature volcano. Something about it had worn off on him, it seemed. I'd never seen him so fluttery, and cooking usually calmed him. He kept jumping up to bring out one more thing until Mother finally said to him, "Austin, you're acting like an idiot. Will you just sit down."

He was halfway out of his chair. "I'll just ask Jenny to join us," he said, nodding as he said it. "It's awkward for her sitting by herself in the kitchen."

"No!" my mother hissed. "Leave it. Leave the poor girl alone!"

He hardly looked up after that, despite the praise.

"It's good, Dad."

"It's delicious," said Claire.

"Very very rich," said Katheryn. "All chocolate, isn't it, dear?"

"There's chocolate in here?"

"Of course, Frances. The sauce is almost all chocolate. That's what I was telling your father."

"Asking," said Gus.

Katheryn laughed. "We can all look forward to adolescent complexions in the morning."

In the middle of the salad Claire brought up the jack-in-the-pulpits. It was only the second time she'd spoken since we sat down. She told a little story about finding the flowers for the first time in the woods behind her house, and eating a dozen of them on a dare. "They looked so frightening. All the kids stood around me after I ate the first one and waited for me to die."

"But you didn't," said Katheryn.

"You grew up in New England, Claire?" asked Gus.

She shook her head. "Illinois. But the country's a lot like this. The same flora and fauna."

"But flatter," I said.

"A little flatter."

"Buggier?" asked Katheryn.

Claire said, "I don't know about buggier."

"But wetter," said Katheryn. "It must be wetter. You don't find jack-in-the-pulpits around here."

"They're all over the place, Kat." Gus was making a pretzel of his napkin. "I sent Fru out to see them this afternoon. By the swamp, and near where the fence used to be, by the Marshalls' place."

"My word. I guess I've never seen a jack-in-the-pulpit in the flesh. Such a city girl. Did you grow up in the city, Claire? They're such fairy-tale flowers."

"I've never thought of them as flowers," said Claire. "They're creatures to me."

"Which reminds me, Austin. You can't guess what

76

Rapunzel brought home this evening. She literally greeted me at the door with the most enormous woodchuck. Frances, right after supper go scoop that out of sight, dear. She's awfully lucky to be alive."

"What news about Britta?" asked Gus.

"Goodness! I can't believe I haven't told you. I've been on the run since this morning. They operated today."

"What do you mean they operated today? Who operated? Why didn't you call me? Why didn't they let you stay with her?"

"It was my choice." Katheryn picked up her empty salad plate and weighed it in her hand. "Hospitals make me absolutely ill. And I didn't call you because I didn't need you, and neither did she. She was under. She was out. It's really a very simple operation, Austin. The doctor assured me."

"God*damn*it, Katheryn. No operation is simple. Not when you're seventy-six years old. Not at any age." He pushed himself out of his chair. "Where's that timetable?" he asked. "Don't we have a current timetable in this house?"

"You're not going in tonight, darling."

"I'll take the earliest train in in the morning."

As he was leaving us, his pocket caught the corner of the table. On his face came a look of such frustration, such defeat, I was certain as he stood there trying to untangle himself he would boil over or break down and cry. Then on his way out he brushed too close to the lamp so the shade swung and the light whitened his white hair. "God-*damn*it," he said, putting a hand up to protect his face. Katheryn turned toward him then. Claire, who had been watching, turned away.

"He's gotten very bad," said Katheryn after he'd left the room. "I put that lamp there yesterday and forgot to tell him. He just doesn't see things anymore."

After supper Claire and I walked to the edge of the woods behind the house and she told me, "Franny, I've

77

got to get out of this madhouse." She was carrying the woodchuck by the neck this time, all its pliability gone. The ground sounded like a drum beneath us.

When we came back, Katheryn sat stiffly at Gus's place at the table, feeding artichoke hearts to the battered terrier in her lap. Jenny had gone off to bed in the room behind the kitchen, and Claire would take the floor in Mother's study. We stood there, my friend and I, in the doorway of my room while I loaded her with a pillow and blankets, her makeshift bed for the night. Behind me my bright yellow canopy bed, my travel posters, even the clothes in my closet made me feel like an émigré from childhood, come as far as the door but no farther.

"Do you love me, Claire?"

She nodded.

"Sleep here with me then."

She opened her mouth but the only sound that came from her was a long, soft *puh*. It seemed to empty her of everything.

Later, alone in my bed, I was woken by the sounds of union which I had always needed to close out but never could, those rare nights of sex between my parents. It was the hardest sex to believe, their bodies only black shadows in my imagination and their faces the faces of dogs, snapping at each other, caressing with their jaws; her sharp face, always the one to take him to bed, and his sad one. This night their whining and whimpering came from everywhere but the room above me. Were they roaming the house? Their breathing came to me through my open door. It seemed to settle in the kitchen, odd place for it, and I thought of Claire on her back in the dark, also kept awake by it. Or did she strain to hear it? I couldn't know.

I longed to go to her, but let my imagination take me there instead. She was the waves, the very belly of them, and this was some hot Massachusetts summer night. Out my window I flew. I raced across the top of the sand to where the beach became the heady white foam of breakers, retreating or coming on. I was eight or twelve or twenty, the same, with the same restless feet running in place on the shore's edge, the same war of voices saying stay or go. And I went. I stripped in a second if I was dressed at all, throwing my shirt and shorts up the beach, my body into the waves. If they had a bulge and belly to them, that was what I swam to, to be inside of. If they curled I wanted to feel the beginning of that on my neck, and the end the whole length of my body.

I left my bed and went to her. I went to her doorway. The blankets came to her waist and her hands covered her breasts. There was nothing to keep me from her but the sudden horrifying thought, *Up and come dance with me.* Even my arms were pitched the same way his had been, pushing out against the doorframe. If she wakes and sees me . . . but I didn't finish the thought. Claire heard or smelled or somehow sensed my presence, though it wasn't me she sensed, it was an old ghost. I only had time to say her name before her mouth fell open on the intake of a scream that never came out of her. It buried itself in her throat and chest and all through her shuddering body.

We sat up all night, listening to the life of the pipes in that house, the elaborate voices of heating and plumbing. We didn't talk. We didn't make love or want to. I remember caressing Claire's head for a long time until she fell asleep, then woke, then slept again with her cheek against my bare thigh. I watched the hours go around on the face of the electric clock, and I was back in my own bed a few minutes before my father came down in his city clothes to wake me.

79

4

All spring in the city we kept to ourselves. I spent every night at Claire's place, and every weekend. The rest of my time I gave to the hamsters. No one bothered us. Between us we had only one friend. Her name was Lydia, and Claire had found her years ago. She was a tall, handsome black woman, a poet and founder of the South Houston Literary Society for Single Women. Claire and I made up the other two-thirds of the membership. We agreed from the beginning that three was as large as we wanted to go.

We used to sit out on the roof in the lawn chairs I'd donated to the house, while Lydia read her poems. They were long and windy, but wild in a way I'd never heard before. She wasn't careful about language, and once I asked her if I could read a few of them over to myself but she just laughed. "Sweetness, you couldn't make head or tail of what's here on the page. I never did learn to spell, and punctuation always went right by me."

Claire said, "If you pause when you read it, put a comma there. If you stop, put a period."

But there wasn't much to be done for Lydia's punctuation, nor did it matter. Half the poetry was in her voice, and the other half was in the sitting out under the stars after sunset with the light noise of traffic below us and maybe a helicopter above us, or a jet. They were dim stars, city stars. Lydia read by flashlight unless the moon was good, and then she read by the moon. She was from Waycross, Georgia, by way of the Women's State Penitentiary in Binghamton, New York. She had the soft, lazy accent of the Deep South, toughened and almost wrenched from her by a hard, convict's drawl. But when she got going, what was really in her poured out of her. I could close my eyes and smell the sweet, perfumed tea olive trees she wrote about. I could imagine the blood-colored back of the cardinal—the redbird who haunted Lydia, heart and mind and eye. Her favorite poet was Wallace Stevens. "That Mr. Stevens goes right by me about ninety-nine percent of the time," she'd say, "but that other one percent, it runs so deep in me I just feel like getting up out of my chair and thanking that man." This meant a lot coming from Lydia, who had a hundred reasons stored in her head for not thanking any man.

Claire had come across her on the street somewhere. They had once waited for a bus together, I think. "How romantic! How exotic!" I shouted at my friend. This was before I met Lydia, whom I considered to be an intruder from Claire's past.

"It wasn't romantic or exotic, Franny. It was raining. We were never lovers. You can relax."

But I began to suspect her of favoring the oddball in all her relationships. I thought about who else she'd come across on the street, or just off it, in Rizzoli's bookstore, and wondered if I wasn't just one of Claire's bag ladies with a little intimacy thrown in on the side. But when Lydia finally arrived with that surprisingly intimate embrace for *me*, a hello for my friend, and an "Oh my, I *know* I know you" with her face up close to mine, I felt the demon leave me for a while and I let myself dig in and love her like Claire did.

She was startling. A tall Afro, a thrice-broken nose in an otherwise perfect face. Strong cheeks, round lips, a few curling chin hairs. In her dark purple undershirt her breasts hung down like eggplants. She had just the beginning of a belly that made her more beautiful for some reason. She always wore the same undershirt and the same pair of plaid pedal pushers, black high heels and knee-highs.

"You're clashing," Claire would tell her.

"Sweetcake," said Lydia, "you get yourself locked up for seven years wearing someone else's blues and light blues all the time, and you got a right to clash. You're happy to clash. Why, in there, you'd give your eyeteeth to have something not go with something else. Show you're alive!"

She was older than Claire, or prison had aged her beyond what thirty or even thirty-five ought to look like. That spring she came to visit every payday and brought with her a couple of quarts of Miller High Life and a bag of pretzel sticks. Also the Wallace Stevens. Claire had given her his *Complete Works,* and that had been the book to get her started. We'd climb to the roof, Claire and I carrying the chairs and Lydia in charge of beer and pretzels, and poetry, and the purse she always toted with her. Wherever she went that purse was there between her feet, a black patent-leather lump with a gold handle and clasp. And one time, after she'd put everything she had, her whole singing voice into Claire's favorite, "The Man on the Dump," she bowed her head to her breastbone and let it hang so still for a few minutes I was sure she'd died. When she came out of it she leaned over her shoes and said in a dreamy voice, "I got something for you ladies." She undid the clasp on the pocketbook and pulled out two china dolls' heads. They had identical painted faces with different colored hair. Each head was the size of a softball.

"If taking from the trash is stealing," she said, "I stole these." Lydia worked in a shirt factory and had easy access to the alleys. "You see how the eyes don't blink? They got no lids. Now what I think is some poor kid got spooked is what I think." She drank some beer. "Some kid couldn't stand his dollies staring at him all day and night and just popped the heads off."

It was an odd story, a little boy with a violent streak offing his dollies. It might have been the truth, though probably not, but how could this matter? Wherever they came from, the heads were ours, and Claire and I kept them in the fruit bowl for a long time, eyes down so we wouldn't have to be seen by them.

Sometime in June Lydia missed a visit. When she came the next week she looked sullen, and in the middle of "The Idea of Order at Key West" she put the book in her lap and sobbed.

"What is it, Lydia?" asked Claire and I in unison.

"Oh women, I been in depression. I can't get myself up in the morning, I can't get to work. This is the first time in a week I been out of my nightie." She was shaking her head at Claire. "I don't know, honey, but the month of June just puts my life right up in front of me where I got to see it—if it doesn't kill me first. Like the weather turns in me same as on the outside. Things going too fast, getting rotten, getting hot. It feels like my whole skin's sticking to my collar. My whole life's rotten and it's riding my back. I just can't *be* at this time of year; I just hate to be."

She raised her hands and was crying loudly into them.

83

"Oh Lydia," said Claire. "Sweet Lydia."

Lydia wanted us to undress her, which we did, and dressed her again in a pair of Claire's pajamas. They were winter pajamas because Claire didn't need to keep warm in the summer. They looked almost seductive on her, as they never had on Claire. She was still crying softly when we put her to bed, and Claire played the piano for her and sang a song. It was a song called "It's Lydia Makes the World Go 'Round," a song her mother had sung to her to cure her of the mumps. I'd heard "It's Franny Makes the World Go 'Round" one long night when my friend was trying to pull me out of a fever.

A few hours later Lydia woke up talking. She wasn't delirious, she was angry. She sat straight up against the pillows and took one pillow into her lap and flat-hand slapped it from time to time. She began with what she believed to be the cause of every moment of misery her life had known: her four brothers, her father and her husband, D. J. She described them all to me in the convict's voice with no trace of the soft South in it whatsoever. Claire had heard parts of the story before. It was like other people's stories, people who were always a long way from me, people you would read about in a junk newspaper. From the day she was old enough to feel too much shame to go running to Mama, Lydia's father and brothers had raped her. Eight, nine, ten years old, even before her body became a woman's body—they had forced the little girl out of her. Fourteen, fifteen, sixteen, the five of them had taken their time at her until she was too tall and strong to lie still. And then she married to get away from them. And then the man she married was just like them.

To get away from him she had to have money, and to get money she forged and stole. Then she worked as a prostitute in Atlanta for a few years, which aged her body three times that. "It just about did in my soul, you can believe it," said Lydia. She was rocking in the bed, her

84

knees drawn up to her chest and her long arms around her knees. "But I sure did meet some lovely ladies." Her voice was the soft one now. "And the day I left that and took up forgery again, it was strange. I felt through and through unlucky. And not a week later they found me out and hauled me off to jail, then to prison where I was nothing but fed bad for seven years. Of course they had us believing it was an act of human kindness we were fed at all. Most of us in there never had raised a finger but to protest something inhuman being done to us, mind or body. But when that don't work, honey, that's when you start using your fists. And you train your hands to help themselves to whatever they want, long as it's worth the trouble to steal."

I thought of those men for a long time afterward, and how the whole circle of meanness can't stop once it's started. Lydia stopped coming, but every payday Claire and I still waited for her, a kind of involuntary listening for footsteps that never arrived at our door. Or wingbeats. We called her the Guardian Angel, and on somber days I stared up at a place in the clouds where I thought she might have disappeared. I saw Claire do it, too, one time, her face all blankness, though it might have been only a pigeon that caught her eye.

Living so closely, the two of us were on and off with each other. We barely knew each other and a one-room apartment four stories up was a difficult place to begin. I was all for moving quickly, while Claire was just the opposite. It was strange how we exaggerated ourselves in some ways, as if we were blind to everything in the ordinary and had to stand poles apart or right inside each other to see at all.

Sex was where we stood inside each other. I learned quickly. I became more graceful. In bed I let myself promise impossible things, such as, I will always be with you, I will always love only you. These were not untrue feelings, but they were of the passionate moment. Claire, I later understood, had had enough of those passionate moments come and go in her life to know them as passing, and know that somewhere out there in the arms of the same or another they would renew themselves. She didn't try to put words to the emotions as I did, to keep them from moving on. Instead, she luxuriated in them with her long throat tilted back, her eyes barely closed. Sometimes a sigh came out of her; it terrified me the first time I heard it. Often there was a sudden rush of color upward from her collarbone.

When I made love to her she was never not with me, I'm certain of that. In the beginning we would drag each other to bed almost every afternoon, talking, dreaming aloud, touching. I was still amazed by the softness, hers and mine both. It had something to do with skin, not flesh, because god knows I was boney. Another thing too: We weren't huge people, but together there felt like so much of us. "I know what you mean," said Claire. "Women's bodies are everywhere; not just what fills the space, but the space too. A man seems to come from one place and be one thing. Poor men. No wonder they make miserable ghosts."

And lovers, Claire? Do they make such miserable lovers? But that was something she never talked about and something my demon would never let me ask.

Who she had been before I knew her was still a mystery—her river was unseined, though she had seen mine turn over a hundred times, the way a pond turns over in the right dusk or cool. She gave off something like climate or temperature that made me want to give to her, give everything up from the bottom of me, all my sticks and mud and green, life-bearing mosses. And at first it didn't matter whether she gave anything back to me or not, then later it did.

We often ate out in a little Polish restaurant that re-

86

minded me of Gus's Brooklyn diner. Meals were under three dollars, and every night the chalkboard on the sidewalk advertised a different, though same-tasting special. It was here, bending over our *pierogi* or poppyseed cake that I learned some things about Claire that the closeness of our bed wouldn't allow me to see. We were sitting one night under the television set. Claire was facing it. The TV was a heavy monster, hung up like a blind eye in a corner of the restaurant. The very old man who worked the cash register from ten o'clock till dawn loved its company, though he rarely turned it on. It was enough to have it watching over him, an RCA angel. I was always terrified it would fall on someone, held up as it was by a few frayed wires.

This particular night he was watching an interview with Peter Ustinov, though most of the time he had his back turned to the set. The restaurant was crowded and Claire and I pushed into the corner table to get away from the noise and the smoke. I sat facing the faces, she faced the window and Peter Ustinov. I can't remember what we were talking about, but her eyes kept jumping up to the screen. This was usually my habit, to be distracted in conversation, but for some reason Claire was hit by it that night. Finally I just brought my chair around and watched with her.

"He's a fat man," I said.

"Very fat."

"Do you think that changes the way he sees things?"

"I'm sure it does," she said, "though his fat brings him a vision or philosophy that something else would bring to someone else. I mean a short person could see things the way Ustinov does, just by being short. Or a thin person. Or a dog owner for that matter. You arrive at it your own way."

Ustinov was talking about how, as a young man, he'd been afraid to die. The keeper of the cash register looked up through the noise of forks meeting plates and the subdued joviality of very early morning. He seemed aware of the night stretching out equally on both sides of the hour, and unable to hear what was said on the TV he dropped his head back to his book of crossword puzzles.

I hadn't been paying attention for a few moments when Claire grabbed my hand. "We know this person," she said. Ustinov held both arms out in front of him as if to ward off an invisible attacker. He was demonstrating his relationship to the world.

"What do you mean?"

"Just listen."

He was saying, "I act, to bring myself into life, to involve myself. But behind the actor is someone who can't take on the world—can't or won't, I'm not certain which. I am in here," he touched his thumb to his breastbone, "and it's out there. I observe it. I stand in the audience. I believe I'm a passionate actor, but a truly impassive liver. The world neither disgusts me nor frightens me. It simply doesn't move me, unless I can take on a role and become that."

The interviewer was bald. He had the nervous energy of a weatherman wanting to point out high and low pressure patterns on the wall behind him. But there was no wall. He was sitting in Ustinov's garden, and the roses were blooming in black and white all over the trellises. "And your attitude toward death?" he asked. "How is that different now than when you were younger? Is it different?"

Ustinov wagged his head up and down. "I'm no longer afraid of it. Some people have called it the last solitary event, and I agree with that, but I'm no longer afraid of solitude. I've packed my life with it, with solitude, consciously or not, as a way of getting prepared. And it's odd," he laughed, "I'm almost always with people. I can't seem to get away from them, but with them I have this way of being without them." He leaned close to the interviewer's face and raised his forefinger. "I will say this. I am a terrible man to love."

That was all. It brought back to me some things I'd known about Claire and forgotten since the afternoon of the teapot, and I wondered whether I'd ever have more than a partial understanding of my friend, with the parts I saw clearly always changing to suit what I needed to see at the moment.

"Do you know what I have the way Ustinov has his acting?" she asked.

I shook my head. "Me?" I shrugged. "I really don't know."

She was embarrassed. "Well, not exactly. There is you, yes," she said, "but before you and after you there's something."

"Claire!" I slammed down my water glass. "You're humiliating me, you know that? You're so blind sometimes." She looked at me with absolute surprise.

What she had been referring to was god. Not God, but god; goddess; the her of her, her Claireness. Except for one conversation about Eden, we had never discussed anything tied to church or religion. I only knew that my friend had grown up Catholic and had left that behind. When I moved in with her I became the silent observer to her rituals. Morning and evening meditation, chanting, and odd postures she put herself in to get the blood flowing to certain neglected parts of the body. I had never seen anything like this. I was afraid to ask her what it all meant for fear of breaking some spiritual taboo. And because I didn't ask, Claire didn't tell me. Once she told me that she was one of those kids who wanted to be a nun, but I didn't know kids like that and I couldn't imagine Claire as one of them.

"Oh sure," she said. "In Catholic schools they're everywhere. The shy little brainy girls who still wear their white socks when everyone else has moved on to stockings, that's the usual type."

"Were you?"

She shook her head. "Not that type exactly. I was brainy, but I understood how the world worked, and how little white socks didn't get you where you needed to go. But I had my altar in the closet, just like they did."

"An altar in the closet!"

"Yes, Franny. Seventh and eighth grade was a big time for that. You went down to Laurel's Grocery and got yourself an orange crate and stuck it upside down in the deepest closet in the house. Ours was a winter coat closet and when I prayed I loved to feel my mother's one ratty fur coat brushing the back of my head. There were all kinds of things you could steal for an altarcloth. Mine was a blue baby blanket that the littlest kid missed for a week then forgot about. I made some origami flowers. I got fancy. I liked the clutter. I had a couple of candles, a rosary; I don't remember what else—half a bar of Ivory soap, a dipping bowl of water. I called it holy water. Maybe I called it holy soap too, I don't remember. That year my mother's mother, my Grandmama died, and up in her attic in an old trunk full of stuffed hats and peacock feathers I found the rosewood Buddha, that little statue on the windowsill. Well he sat on my altar for a year. He sat between the origami flowers and the charm bracelet, and the tiny whistle on the charm bracelet had to be just so, next to but not touching the Buddha. The arrangement was very important, Fran. Everyone who had an altar felt this way. I never asked them. Of course you never talked about it to anyone; it was your secret. But you could tell. I could tell by the look of a girl whether she was one of us or not, and we went around knowing who knew, like a little subculture of innocents. And we were happy for each other's unspoken company. We were so secretly, silently happy for that, I can't tell you."

"Did they all become nuns but you?"

"I doubt any of them did. One of them grew up and married the football coach. Another drove her car into a wall, and when that didn't work she shot herself in the mouth. Maybe some grew up and became drug addicts. Maybe we got a couple of dykes out of the bunch." She laughed. "But nuns, I wouldn't count on any of us for nuns. The work's too hard." I saw she was serious. "And the pay's in heaven. And if you can find heaven around all the billboards that advertise the way to heaven, you don't need the convent anyway. You need the world."

You need the world, Claire had said. At the end of the summer I would remember those words and use them against her, but at the time I simply took them in and nodded over what seemed like my friend's sensible approach to spiritual affairs. I was happily areligious myself. Religion had never occurred to me, that was all. Whatever Gus and Katheryn's beliefs were, they had never passed them on to me, and among my friends I never went out looking for god either. Or rather, God, which was the only form of the name I knew before I met Claire.

The first time I watched her meditate I didn't know what I was watching. We had just begun to live together and those mornings I woke up enchanted in her bed, feeling impatient with desire for her. Claire lay stretched beside me on top of the sheets. No matter where we began the night before, it seemed by morning she would have whatever was on her thrown off her. She was still asleep. Her head was turned to the side and the wet spot of saliva on the pillow brought out my tenderest feelings for her; something softer and warmer than sexual. I woke her up kissing her, as I often did, but this time she pushed me away.

"Unh-unh," she rolled her head back and forth. I thought she was playing or dreaming, and I pressed my lips and my face into her hair. "I don't *want* that." She brought her elbow up and caught my jaw. I sat straight up, rubbing it.

"What do you mean you don't want that? You've always wanted it before, a little affection in the morning."

"Well, I don't want it now," she said. "I'm sleeping." But her eyes were open and she lay still on her side for a very long time.

I thought she might be sick. "Claire?" I had been up making toast and tea, and I had eaten my breakfast sitting in front of the window, watching a thin skirt of pollution lift up out of the city. It hung over us now so I was watchful of each breath I took, and my breathing became longer, stronger, steadier. "Claire?" She didn't answer. I turned to look at her. "Claire, are you alive? Say something. No? Tap your hip if you'd like to say something but aren't ready to yet. Are you there?"

I finally got up and went to her, and she frightened me, lying so still, staring at the wall. I rolled her onto her back and she was so pliable I was horrified.

"You feel like you've lost your bones!"

"I'm just relaxed. I was meditating."

"That's how you meditate? You lie down and face the wall?"

"I usually sit up and face the wall, but I didn't think I could do that with you here."

I was stunned. I was aware of an unwelcome voice inside me that cried, So this is the door she will shut to shut you out.

We didn't talk any more about it. Not then, or ever. Claire found a way around my presence in the room to go through her rituals twice, sometimes three times a day. And every time she went through them I felt a strange homesickness that had nothing to do with family or place, Gus and Katheryn in New Jersey. My stomach ached as if I'd eaten the wrong food. My throat ached and tightened. I looked at my friend where she sat, and I thought I could see the lines that held her together, like some faraway bridge I loved for its correct use of tension. The tension enhanced the physical, and I always wanted to touch her then but never did, because I knew she wouldn't allow it. If she were sitting cross-legged on the floor with her back to me, her back would be more beautiful than I'd ever seen it. Or if she were up in a headstand or balancing on one foot, or prostrating herself in front of the little wooden Buddha, I'd wonder who this woman was, this compelling being, and why she had to leave me to be with me.

We were making the bed together one day when I told her about this homesickness, only I called it love. She shrugged and said too quickly, "You always want a person most when they're looking away, that's all."

"I said love, Claire, not want."

"But you meant want, didn't you, Franny?"

I might have meant want. It didn't matter. Something had happened to the sex in our lives and I wanted what Claire didn't want almost all the time. And because I couldn't have it it was everywhere. Sex was in the sheets, in our clothes, in the sheer and billowy curtains I'd hung to shade our window. Any spot of dampness brought it to me, and after Claire went to work I would push my face into the towel she'd just dried herself with. Or it would come to me on the streets, the little cracks of sidewalk filled with grass, the ginkgo trees' gray-green fluttering above my head. Wind would bring it to me, quick gusts that blew the litter against buildings or legs; loud, sudden wind in the alleys I walked, often only to hear it, to see how it toppled the trash cans. They were long walks, often after dark, always alone. This was how I made love to myself those times when Claire wouldn't. I sent the river back underground. It gathered itself. It wanted again and more.

Sex brought us back to Gus one evening. Or rather, Emily Dickinson brought us back and sex followed us there. It was mid-June, already stiflingly hot in the city. Our restaurant was deserted at ten o'clock because most of the clientele could be cooler at home. The two big ceiling fans barely pushed the air ahead of them, and the air itself had an almost visible thickness and weight. Our old man had been carried away to a nursing home and his replacement was a tall, sluggish teenage boy who watched so much television that the regular customers had complained of the noise. Now a mirror hung where the TV used to be, and the boy spent his time looking up at it, running his fingers across his acne.

Claire's apartment had no cross-ventilation and only a tiny, inadequate rotating fan that we joked about. Every time I threatened to pawn it she thought of a new use for it. "Wait, Franny, we'll see if it slices carrots," or cuts hair, or sharpens pencils. Most of the summer it just stood before the tall windows, singing its whirr to the birds.

So we were happy for even that sluggish cool of the Polish palace, and the sweaty boy at the cash register was a study in adolescence at least. This particular evening we were very fond of each other. Earlier that day Claire had hopped a barrier at the Bronx Zoo to bring me the newly shed feather of a snowy egret. I had watched her run a few yards across the tundra, laughing, scattering birds and zebras to pick up her prize. Now I wore it in my hair and pulled it out to play with while she traveled back to that late-March kitchen where my father had plied her with Emily Dickinson.

"He doesn't know a thing about poetry," she said. Gus hadn't made his way into any of our conversations of the past several weeks, until that moment. "He's a charlatan, Franny. He's a doddery old man masquerading as a play-boy."

"Claire!"

"It's true, Fran. I hadn't meant to say it but I won't take it back. It's not so terrible either, or unusual. He just doubts his virility, that's all, so he surrounds himself with women who adore him."

"That's crazy, Claire, he loves women. What's the matter with a man who loves women?"

"But he doesn't love women, sweetface. It's the old story—he needs them to love him because he's too afraid to love himself. I don't know if he's always been this way, but these days he's so afraid of dying he can't even live right."

"He loves Britta," I said, "and he loves me."

"Britta he seems to love, but you he's mystified by."

"What makes you say that?"

"He said it."

This surprised me. I'd never tried to imagine what Gus and Claire had talked about after I left them that afternoon to track down the jack-in-the-pulpits. "What else did he say?"

"He denied things."

"What kind of things?" I groaned. I could see Gus, head bent over the cookbook, intent on his chicken *molé* while Claire battered him with questions—or worse, accusations.

"He denied that remembering is more healthy than forgetting."

"That's because Gus remembers too much. He can get very nostalgic."

Claire shook her head. "A different kind of remembering. More like awareness. Total involvement. It doesn't lean on the past like the other kind does."

"And you talked to my father about this?"

"I told him I felt my courage was being tested every moment. How as a kid I was always inventing tortures for myself, real and imaginary, to get myself stronger so I wouldn't give in when it really mattered."

"You mean when you were taken prisoner of war or something?"

Claire laughed. "Something like that. It was never very clear to me what or when the real test would be, which of course made every moment the real test. I once held myself under in the horse pond. This was March, and

March can be awfully cold in Illinois. The ice had just broken up on the larger lakes. I went in with my clothes on. I had my heavy boots on. I even wore my hat. I ducked under and made myself count a hundred."

"A hundred!"

"And while that was going on I was sure it was the real test, until it was over and I knew, before I even got out of that pond I knew I'd have to test myself again, go out and eat scary looking mushrooms, stick my arm into some creature's hole. But if I could remember that every test was the real test, that every moment was, a strange thing happened. It happens now. It's like time gets wider, or blossoms. You know when something takes you by surprise, Franny, or a certain amount of pain will do this to you. There's suddenly nothing else in the world but that." I nodded. "That's the kind of remembering I was trying to talk to your father about. I talked while he cooked. That's the way it was that afternoon. We'd start in on something like this, or poetry, and he'd say what he thought and I'd disagree with him. We disagreed on just about everything. But as soon as I'd start to argue he'd just clam up and pretend to lose himself in his cooking. Didn't you ever say no to your father? He can take it from your mother, why can't he take it from anyone else?"

"And that makes him a charlatan?" I was stroking my white feather flat on the Formica tabletop. The Formica was a dirty white with gold flecks in it, and now ringed with the marks of Claire's coffee cup. We were alone, except for the boy who was searching through the funnies, jiggling one knee over the other with his foot up on the rung of the stool.

"He's masturbating," Claire said. "See that?" She tilted her head in his direction. "The young man's getting it off."

"Shh. . . . You mean, getting it on."

"On, off? Who cares? Getting queer with himself,"

she said. "Look at his face, Franny. Why, he's just a kid, isn't he?"

I couldn't look at him the way Claire could. He *was* just a kid, but not that much younger than me, after all. And the way he half closed his eyes as the jiggling continued seemed a kind of plea for privacy, though he had no idea two women were watching him.

"No, that doesn't make him a charlatan," said Claire, so suddenly I had to think back for a moment to who the "him" was. "But something else does."

"What's that?" I asked.

"Jenny," she said. She said it with a finality that made me have to prod her for more.

"Go on."

"Gus was completely taken with her. He was nuts about her—infatuated. If not for the presence of his daughter, and the annoying presence of his daughter's friend, he would have chased that poor woman around the table."

"What table?" I asked dumbly.

"It doesn't matter what table, Franny. He was after her. Gus was after her. And that, to me, makes him a charlatan."

My first reaction, which they say is the true one, the instinctive one, was, Of course he was taken with her, a beauty like that. I was too. But this was quickly covered with disbelief: Claire must be a liar. And then finally, embarrassment, when I thought back to those muffled sounds of copulation coming, that night, not from my parents' room above me but from the kitchen, Jenny's little room behind the kitchen.

I was too raw to hear anything else and Claire knew this. Anyway, she had said more than she'd ever intended. She could have said it months ago. We sat for a while in the restaurant, needing its blandness. Claire ordered iced tea for both of us before we went home for the night. I wanted to tell her how I felt, so I told her about being a very young child at the planetarium and staring into a display case that showed the earth in relation to the entire galaxy. There was a button you pushed and the earth lit up red, an infinitesimally small dot amidst all that hubbub of stars. I remember every time somebody pushed it I would peer up, hoping the earth had grown or the galaxy had shrunk, and every time this didn't happen I would squeeze my eyes shut, and chew my fist and cry.

5

July, where we lived, was a violent month. Two lovers killed each other one afternoon in a dispute over a sandwich. A little boy drowned in the street. Claire and I were awakened one night by the hollow, rushing sound of a train, followed by two explosions, and as we watched, smoke and fire sucked out the ground floor windows of the building across from hers.

"It's so willing," said Claire.

"What's so willing?"

We stood with nothing on in front of the windows.

"That building—the wood and paper and plaster of it."

"To be destroyed?"

She nodded.

Willing or not, it took all night to go, and we were mesmerized by the destruction: The sudden eruption of ladders and the hacking of brick and timber as the firemen clawed their way inside; the tall, intersecting arcs of water; the steam's noise; its smell; a sharp rain of glass in the street, followed by a woman or child's shriek. We watched as strangers, not as neighbors, until we climbed to the roof and felt the shock of heat on our faces and saw each other in the weird glow of the flames. I took Claire's hand. By morning the building was a gutted steel skeleton whose only flesh hung from a fourth-floor apartment: a window shade in its window, and behind that the remains of a bed. "The withered arm," Claire said, pointing, and I saw this was where he had lived, his lair.

The destruction was in us, too, in Claire's demand for more and more solitude, and in my jealousy, my easily aroused demon. I accused her of loving others, of loving men, of loving herself above all.

"You have no idea who I've loved, and you wouldn't care to."

"What does that mean, Claire?"

"You won't let yourself."

"Let me worry about that," I said. "Try me. Tell me something."

"Ask me something."

"Who was the first one? How did it start?"

"The first one was my brother," she said. "He was passing by my window on the hottest day of the summer and his arms were full of burlap sacks."

"Claire! I don't believe you."

"Behind him on the road the trucks were hauling alfalfa. It must have been early July. I was about to be fourteen, so he was thirteen, just. He was carrying the sacks up to my mother, who was killing the old hens that day."

"I don't care about the old hens, Claire. You tell me you fucked your brother. Why would I care about the hens?"

"From my window I could see her dipping the bodies into a pot of steamy water. Her hands were red to the wrist, I do remember that. She dipped a couple, then hung them by the feet from the clothesline. That way she had both hands free for plucking and she moved very fast. She unskirted them. That was her word for it, 'unskirted.' If there were any breeze at all, the feathers would fly up from the pile and stick to the hens all over again, and when she had a dozen hens hanging she'd take the hose to them and call me out for gutting."

Claire looked up at me. Her mouth was a tight, thin line. "You asked, Franny. Just be happy you asked.

"It was an attic window. I'd go up there to be alone. There was a bed up there and I'd lie on it and masturbate. After that I'd do a little ceremony, like saying a certain thing as I hopped on my right foot, then switching feet and saying something else. They were incantations, I guess, to keep the bad off me."

"What bad?" I took hold of her arm. "Go on," I said. "I'm right here with you."

"The bad that was all around me. The bad that only an altar in a closet or a secret attic ritual could protect me from. I felt the protection. Sometimes it felt like actual hands touching me. And in the summer the heat in the attic set me in a kind of trance that I loved. I saw things in that state—ecstatic visions, I called them. I guess I believed I had a better shot at sainthood than most of my friends."

"What did *that* mean?"

"Oh, dear Franny, of course I didn't know what it meant, or what anything meant. I was just feeling, that's all. This was where I let myself feel."

"Then why did your brother come into it? Aren't sainthood and chastity all tied up in a knot?"

Claire nodded. "That's exactly why Troy came into it. We were the same flesh. Sex with him would be like sex with myself, and that was something I was full of that summer. I didn't know the social taboo—"

"And he didn't either?"

"My world wasn't midtown Manhattan, Fran. I watched the animals. I wasn't too young to know shame, I just didn't know that what I was doing was something to be ashamed about."

"And he didn't either?"

Claire closed her eyes. She nodded slowly. "Yeah. I think he did."

"And this is the brother who calls you whenever he gets into trouble? This is the brother who keeps you away from your precious sleep? Your father kept you awake nights, too, didn't he, Claire?"

"You can stop now."

"But this one, this lover of yours, why hasn't he called since I've lived here? Does he know you're living with a woman? What does he call about? His troubled marriage? Whether he should go for a walk or beat his wife? And what do you tell him, friend? What's your wise counsel? God, I hate to think whose side you're on.

"I can just imagine it. Let me, Claire. You're at the window. You're thirteen. Your sweet little face is pressed against the screen, all longing, all innocence. Those big eyes of yours. And you say to him, 'Come up here, Troy, and show me how to fuck.' Is that what you say to him, Claire? Is that the way you say it? You have to almost shout it, don't you, baby? He's down there and you're up here. Not loud enough for *her* to hear it, the old hen killer, but enough to make him drop his sacks, or whatever the hell they really are and climb up to you. On the rope of your hair. Did you make a fairy-tale rope of your hair? Or did he start it? Did he come find you in the attic with your hand between your legs and convince you he had a better way? I can just see him, just like you but the animal of you, coming out of the shadows with his pants down and rubbing an old clove of garlic on a string around his neck —"

"Franny!" She tried to clamp her hand across my mouth but I pushed her onto the floor.

"Don't try and stop me, Claire. Did you try and stop him? Did he tell you the garlic was a good luck charm? It would keep your sex sacred—*if* you didn't tell a soul?" She was sobbing. My friend was curled in a ball, crying into her hands. "If I'm wrong, I want to know it," I said.

"You're wrong."

"But he was the bad that was all around you, wasn't he, Claire?" She didn't answer. "He still is, isn't he, Claire?"

She said something I couldn't hear and when I leaned down to hear it I took her into my arms.

This was one of our battles; every day brought us others, and only after each battle could we love each other. Physical acts of meanness, and even violence, precipitated our lovemaking where no kindness could have. Something would break in the world of objects: A rosewood chip would fly off the Buddha where I hurled it against the wall; a fist would come down, a bruise would rise. Once I crushed Claire's hand in a door, and in our relief that nothing was fractured we found ourselves in bed, laughing because all through our caresses she had to hold the hand up like a flag to slow the swelling. This seesawing between passions. I never knew what I would wake up to, or who would inhabit my body from hour to hour, or the body of my lover.

Her solution was to spend some time apart. "We spend our days apart," I said.

"Our nights then."

But I refused not to be with her. She began to stay out late, eventually all night, and while these were terrible times for me, I saw, one evening, what had become of her. She had been gone for a few days. We had argued one morning and she hadn't come home. She hadn't even come in as she usually did after I left for work, leaving the signs of herself that let me know she'd passed through: a dish out of place, an exchange of clothes in the closet. Without knowing it, I had become fastidious in my housekeeping in order to keep track of her. When I stepped into a room where Claire had been, I could feel her there, her calm or hurry. The missing egg shouted of her, the one less than the seven I'd counted that morning. Or the dampness of the shower I hadn't taken. Or her hairbrush—I didn't look for the new hairs lost to it, or have to. I had a sense of her having picked it up, generously stroking herself the way I would have loved to, and at times like that my fury and jealousy and pity, all three, went out to her.

I wondered what she did in the streets, where she went, whether she leaned on car hoods to eat a dry, ham salad sandwich and drink a lonely milk. I didn't know her friends. I no longer let myself imagine her with lovers, though my mind sometimes put her in a strange bed with darkness, and I was immobile for the few seconds it took to will that absence of light away.

When Claire was with me, we liked to sit in the window in the late afternoon, or go up to the roof and watch the day city vanish and the night city come up like stars. This was our favorite hour. Claire called it the hour of estrangement, when the details dissolved and the stuff of things wavered in the dusk. As if everything were deciding how to be. The buildings had lost their names; they could not be distinguished, nor defined yet by their lights. Traffic was all one noise, through which shone each shrilling of horn or brake. The insults and affections that rose from the street below us were all one, were the one voice deep and booming, high and sharp, that our hearing was filled with or emptied of, until the darkness became sure and in the next moment the hour was over. We loved that time. We had it to ourselves. We seldom argued at dusk.

If she hadn't come home yet, I always expected her then. I knew how she softened at that time of day, and how her softness would always bring her back. This was my third afternoon without her. I was drowsy in the heat and dozing by the window, waiting for dusk and hoping to wake to Claire. Down on Thompson Street some kids had opened up a fire hydrant and were playing in front of it, more cautiously now since the drowning death of their friend.

For some reason that death had moved Claire. "He died in a few inches of water, Franny. Doesn't that bother you?"

"People die in their sleep," I shrugged.

"But he wasn't asleep. He had some say in the matter."

"And he said yes. And you can't understand why he didn't say no."

She was quiet a minute. "No. I just never realized that when you got a good close look at it it could look that good."

"Maybe it just looked better than what he was used to," I said. "Not every kid walks around happy inside." But Claire wasn't listening.

Now I could hear their hooting and shouting, sharpened by the dull rush of water from the hydrant. Half of me listened. Half of me dreamed. I had no idea then, and still don't, what made me sit up all of a sudden and look out the window, but there was Claire, rounding the corner from the subway. She was carrying a grocery sack, but instead of coming home she was walking very slowly toward the group of kids around the fire hydrant. Even from that distance I could see the armpits of her shirt darkened by those half moons of sweat that I loved. She seemed to be carrying an extraordinary weight, though it had nothing to do with the sack which she held lightly in one hand so it swung back and forth of its own momentum. As I watched, she staggered, misjudging the sharpness of the curb as she started across the street. I had never seen Claire stagger before. Some of the boys gave up their teasing and fighting to stare at her. They were white-chested young boys in soaked shorts or blue jeans. The girls wore two-piece bathing suits and the older ones had beach towels wrapped around their waists. They were playing a game of limbo, using the jet of water from the hydrant as a pole.

"*Jesus!*" I heard one of the kids shout over the steady pound of the water. Claire had reached the middle of the street and a light blue delivery truck was bearing down on her. It was an odd shape, low to the ground and with no doors. The driver honked and accelerated, and he reached his arm out as he passed and slapped her hard on the ass. She spun around and kicked at the back of the truck, but it was almost halfway down the block by then. I thought I could hear the high, whinnying laugh of the driver.

He's probably sniffing the hand he hit her with, I thought. Oh my poor Claire. He won't wash it until he goes home and touches his wife.

Claire dropped the grocery sack in the street and kicked away her shoes. She took a few steps toward the kids who had cleared away from the hydrant and now stood in a silent half-circle behind it. She didn't seem to see them. She didn't seem to see anything but the tunnel of water slapping the pavement in front of her and jumping up again in a hard white spray. She let the water drop onto her bare feet, wetting her pants leg. She took another step and the water rose to her knees. It parted around her. The next step brought her only a few feet from the hydrant itself, and the water flailed out in all directions as it hit her body. It looked like white sparks or crazy snakes, hitting her thighs and flying up her chest, leaping from her shoulders and chin. She bent her legs a little and leaned back, as if she were part of that limbo game.

"Why, Claire, why?" I whispered.

By now some of the kids were clapping and the movement moved their whole arms. They elbowed each other and rocked their shoulders, and the girls let their hips come into it. There was energy down there, I realized.

There was almost a joy. I felt my own body loosen up for a split second, and all that was held back in me, these days, these weeks of wanting, relaxed and gave way. And froze again, because there on the street, as I watched, Claire's shirt tore off her. It was a green cotton, I remember noticing for the first time, and the force of the water sent it up over her face. She put her hands up to stop it—it looked like a sickly skin she was peeling from her—but it swept back over her head and down her back, and the water quickly carried it into the gutter.

I thought she would run and pick up the grocery sack and wear it home, but she only pressed farther into the spray, so it covered her more completely; it became her spumy costume. Maybe she wanted to hide in it until dark. But I knew her legs and chest must ache from the force of it. She wouldn't be able to stand up much longer. I saw her bend her head to the mouth of the hydrant as if she were bowing to it or looking for something in the water. The water boiled over the top of her head and across her naked back until suddenly it seemed to cave in around her and she sank or was carried to her knees.

A minute went by. I could see her slumped against the hydrant, under the mouth of it, but she didn't move. One of the girls wearing a beach towel over her bathing suit caught the arm of the girl beside her who was pointing at Claire. She undid the towel in front of her friend. She flapped it open then shut again, bending one knee across the other in a calendar pose. They held on to each other, laughing.

Another minute, and then I watched Claire crawl around behind the hydrant and use it to pull herself up. When she stood up I felt I'd never seen her breasts before. They were a deep red, and her neck was red, and though I wanted not to, I remembered that rush of color that covered her neck and breasts in sex, the flush that told me without her telling me that she felt my touch, her pleasure, all over her body. She found her shirt in the gutter and tried to cover herself with it, to cover each breast with a shred of it, but it was useless. One of the boys started punching his fists in the air, then beating his chest. I couldn't hear anything over the water's noise but I could see his gestures become more animated as he turned to his friends, and some of them took it up, too, waving their arms and pummeling themselves.

Claire noticed none of this. She held the shirt to her, clutched in a tight ball between her breasts, so it covered nothing. She walked very slowly, with a dreamy, balloon-like grace, across Thompson Street. It was empty of traffic. She was still barefoot, and there were a few men and women on the street who seemed to notice only that, dropping their faces down as she passed between them. Someone else shouted "Baby!" at her. Someone whistled. Halfway home, she threw the shirt to the ground and went on, holding a hand over each breast. At the same time she was looking up at the face she guessed had been watching all this from her window.

"You saw it?" she said. She had let herself in and stood with her forearms crossed on her chest. I didn't move from the window and she leaned back against the door, shutting it.

"Yes, Claire."

"Left my bag and shoes out there."

"Do you want me to get them?"

She shook her head.

"What was in the bag?"

"Don't remember. Maybe nothing. Some cheese. Some money."

"Where did you go?"

"Unh," she shrugged. "Slept out. Slept in a car one night. Met some people. Skipped work. Met a singer. From Hollywood. Had three doors in her pocket and couldn't hit a note with any of them."

Claire's knees were going out from under her. Suddenly she sat right down on the floor.

"Here you go." I went to her and lifted her up. She clung to me. "Here you are." I put her onto the bed and while she talked through her delirium about people she'd never met and things she'd never seen, I undressed her.

"That guy had a wolf provider. . . ."

"Yes, Claire. Quiet now." I turned her on her back and stroked her legs and stomach.

"And a she-ticket. You know a she-ticket, Franny?"

"Mmm, a she-ticket."

"Well, he had one."

"Does this hurt, Claire?" I lay my hands on her welted breasts. Her skin was hot and raw, and I lifted my hands and touched her only with my fingertips. "Does this hurt you, baby? Does anything hurt you?"

I was leaning over her, crying over her. I watched the tears drop onto her strange skin.

"That stings," she said.

I dropped my head down next to hers on the pillow, and while she slept I stroked the parts of her I loved. Hip, throat, the hollow of her knee, the eyelids, made of paper, and the thigh's curve. I held my hand between her thighs for a long time. I felt her heat, and how soft she was under the coarse hair. I started rubbing her, gently playing my fingers around her cunt and clitoris. I moved down her body and kneeled between her knees. She said something in her sleep and tried to roll, but I had a hand on her leg, keeping her. She loved to be licked, and I licked her, slowly, softly. I wanted her to feel me in her dreams.

She woke up shuddering, lifting her ass off the bed and crying out as she came, raw guttural noises that rose in my throat as well as I felt her get harder and harder and softer, her orgasm on my tongue.

"God, Franny!" she gasped. She was rolling her dark head from side to side on the white pillow. There was a tea-colored light in the room at the end of the hour of estrangement.

I brought my hands to her face and held her still. "We haven't loved for a long time, Claire."

"Love," she said. "Love, I *am* so glad we do this for each other."

Our peace was always temporary, often lasting no longer than the sex that brought it on. Or at other times a confession could prolong it, or a childhood memory—anything that gave us back the ground we shared. Claire came home one stifling Saturday afternoon, and as she rid herself of her costume I suddenly noticed how much more ordinary she seemed to me than when I'd first seen her pull the teapot over her head a few months earlier. She wasn't beautiful. I was relieved to discover that. She wasn't anything but Claire. The day had drained all the life and color from her body. Even her hands were pale. She looked frail and disoriented, standing half-naked in the center of the room with the teapot on its side behind her like an egg she'd hatched out of.

"Did I ever tell you my grandmother built a radio?" she asked. I shook my head. "She was seventy-four when she started and it took her two years to finish. I used to sit by her and listen to the different languages coming out of it as she turned the dial. She got Paris and Germany, and a funny kind of English that must have been Australia. I was thinking about her today, and how she brought me the world. It's her birthday. She would have been a hundred."

It was my friend's birthday too. She was thirty-one, and for some reason it moved her. She'd brought a bottle of wine home to celebrate, and we drank it and talked of people who weren't us, and felt cured.

Little Claire in front of that radio is one picture that's stayed with me, almost to haunt me at times. I see the scabby knees swinging from the straight-backed chair, and the scuffed brown shoes that don't quite touch the floor. She is leaning forward, both Claires are. Claire at seven and Claire at thirty-one. The older Claire to kiss me, the younger with her face in a knot, trying to make sense of a babble of German or French. "What's that mean, Grandmama?" but the strange language already gone by and another come to replace it. Like a puzzle her ear can't undo. And in the Brooklyn diner the Yiddish and Polish and Russian all run together so my little girl's ear hears only the river that is all of them. I am so lightheaded I want it to carry me forever, a round river, and perhaps it will. A river as vivid as memory, as distorted as time. Perhaps it has.

I remember only one other of Claire's stories, this one about her mother's tall, thin, tubercular brother who lived in self-imposed isolation somewhere in the mountains of New Hampshire. "Uncle Dickie was a cross between Santa Claus and Sarastro," she told me. "He was an old homosexual—wild looking and charismatic. Later he turned into sort of a monk and took on 'acolytes,' as he called them. He'd have two or three of these young boys in the house all the time, cooking for him, sleeping on boards, up at dawn lighting the incense. And he didn't pay them a cent. Dickie never had any money to give away. Just champagne."

"Champagne!"

"Yeah," Claire nodded. "Whenever the flour and potatoes were gone, and the firewood was down to a few sticks, Dickie would dig all the crumpled singles out of his pocket and send a little boy to town for champagne. And then he'd pour it into a basin and make all the acolytes wash in it. And when they were done washing in it, they'd drink it."

Whether I believed this or not didn't matter. Claire did. And if she invented some of her past, as I sometimes found myself hoping, the inventions were still hers, though the past she described might not be.

There was something about who she was and where she'd been that I was finally ready to know. "Have you loved many men?" I asked her.

"I've loved some men," she said.

"Have you been to bed with them?" She nodded. "Oh, Claire."

"They always made me long for women, Franny."

"Why? Did they hurt you?"

"No one intentionally hurt me," she said. "But when I was with them I gravitated toward their breasts. There was a pull there. I wanted to touch their breasts, and touch them and touch them. As if I could make them women's breasts just by putting my hands over them."

"And could you love a man now?" I asked.

"Only like a brother." She flushed. "I mean I could love a man for being human, Franny, as human as me. That's all."

"Could you love another woman? Do you want to go on and love someone else? I don't love you for the same reason anyone else does, you know that, Claire."

"Which is why I don't love everyone else the way I love you."

"But you've loved other women this way?"

"To love one woman is to love all women. Do you believe that, Franny?"

I didn't, and I told her so, and though there were a hundred more questions I wanted to ask I kept them to myself. I didn't trust her to answer them. That wasn't an answer: To love one woman is to love them all. What I didn't see at the time was that neither was my question a question. None of them were. They were the chance I gave Claire to give me the response I was waiting for, to confirm my hope that ours would be the love that would never fail.

By the end of July I had begun to take everything

personally. If my friend had lunch with someone, I wanted to know who. If someone interested or delighted her, I held it against them. "I resent you for being in love with someone as great as me," I told her, "and then not treating me as the most important thing in your life."

In my stronger moments I could see we were ending, and that this ending was the natural and inevitable one for our relationship. That two people would come together at all seemed such a miracle. Claire echoed this one morning, looking up from *The Lives of a Cell*. "Listen to this, Fran. 'Statistically, the probability of any one of us being here is so small that you'd think the mere fact of existing would keep us all in a contented dazzlement of surprise.'" Life was *for* us, in other words. We were the chosen. Women and women—and men and women—had joined and parted since the day it all began.

But these were only my stronger moments. Most of the time I felt sullen and weak in my heart, and often I hated Claire. This kept me from saying what I wanted to say, shouting "I love you! and if you die without knowing me it won't have been worth it. I'm your heart!" And every time I didn't say it I let her slip away a little more.

Up until then we'd been funambulists, a word Claire had found in the dictionary meaning tightrope walker, approaching each other from opposite ends of the wire. I had learned that by looking at her I could keep my balance better than if I looked at some point above or below her, but Claire's way was to look only a few yards ahead of her own feet. My hope had been that once we got close enough, she, without realizing it, would be looking at *my* feet, and closer still, my legs, until I filled her vision—all of me! Unhappy romantic. It didn't matter now if she'd fallen or risen up—on wings? a current of air? that substance she called her spirit? She was no longer with me on the wire. I had it to myself and didn't want it. I wobbled. I reached for her, and the reaching almost threw me over.

And then one day in early August a letter landed in my lap, describing one half of our future, implying the other. There was a position open at the Bhakti-devi Ashram in the Caroline Islands. Claire was invited to come out. I looked up at her. "I didn't even know you'd applied. Where is this place? What are they, missionaries?"

"I didn't apply, exactly. It's a spiritual community with ashrams all over the world. This one's in Micronesia. I just wrote to them in Oregon and asked for information, and they sent me this."

"Will you go? What will you do there?"

"I don't have any idea."

"But which question does that answer, Claire?" I was up on my knees, pulling at her neck with both hands. I forced her face down close to mine and kissed her roughly, my tongue deep in her mouth, until she caught her balance and pushed me off her. I could hear her take the stairs in two's, the way she always did when she was fleeing from me.

We had a week, then she would be gone for two years. She offered me the chance to take over her apartment, which I refused. She'd already given notice at the museum. As far as family went, I was only aware that she talked to Troy, who was in a detox center somewhere in California.

"Do you want me to leave while you call him?" I asked her.

"Leave? No, Franny, you don't have to leave."

"Aren't there things you want to say to him that you'd hate me to hear?"

"Such as what?"

But I couldn't tell her. I didn't know myself. I only remembered the first time I talked to Claire on the telephone, how soft and deep her voice had been, and how I'd never wanted to hear her use that voice for anyone else.

What few possessions she had, Claire gave away to friends, most of whom I'd never met before. It was odd, riding around with her in a borrowed station wagon, unburdening ourselves of what I considered to be the details of our life together, both bitter and sweet. How easily they fell to strangers. A few clothes, books and the Buddha she packed in a trunk to take with her to the islands. The piano would stay for the next occupant, and on my insistence we kept the bed with us until the end instead of carting it off to someone's loft for firewood. All the worldly work and busyness of those days might have been good for me, though I resented it at the time. It did numb me. It prepared me. It even allowed me, our last night together, to laugh at a spectacle I never would have predicted. Claire's apartment was bare of everything but the bed, piano, and a sawed-off broom handle she'd used all summer to prop open the top of the teapot for ventilation. The rest of that costume had gone to the garbage, though neither of us had actually seen it into the truck. My feeling was that the next to need it had picked it up and walked away with it. Claire was sure whoever it was had walked away inside it.

The broom handle was the length of Claire's arm. For some reason that evening she picked it up and carried it with her as we walked around doing the last minute cleaning. I was quiet. So was she. Then all of a sudden she started tossing and catching the stick. It was nothing fancy at first, just an old talent she was on the edge of remembering. But with each toss she added a twist or a spin to it, and her body worked faster and faster until finally she was pure motion in the center of the floor—elaborate motion. I sat on the bed and my eyes could barely keep up with her.

She was concentrating hard. I could hear her breathing, though the windows were open and the night city came loudly through them. The sweat gleamed on her face. She laughed from time to time, a short, almost snort, and I did too. But no words. Only the rising and sinking baton.

She tried a triple spin, but the stick dropped. She picked it up and tried again, and dropped it again. The third time the stick went up, she must have flung it higher, or perhaps she spun faster, because she went three times around and caught it in her hand. I was watching her face, which was three different faces, one, two, three, each time she turned. And none of them was the Claire I knew, and none of them was meant for me.

"I don't think I'm afraid of being left alone," I told her in bed that night.

"You won't be alone for long."

"I'm afraid I'll never be able to love somebody else as well."

"As me?"

I nodded. "And I'm afraid I'll lose my touch, never learn as much again. Never *feel* as much again. Claire! you're so precious to me now. What if I forget this!" I rolled to her and grabbed her with a force that surprised us both.

TWO

6

Sadness has its own momentum, and after Claire left I lived like a shadow all day, and all night lay heavy and sleepless, as if I were packed with clay. I remembered too much, such as Claire smoothing me down one night of a fever, laughing, telling me my body was like a bag of stones. Telling me, enough hard things together feel soft. Making no sense through my delirium. I wasn't even aware until now, months later, that the words had lodged in me. Or Claire, dreaming up names for things to change the way we looked at them: Bob was the Christian God she grew up with; death was a table; life a chair. Everywhere I looked, in my room in my parents' apartment at night, in the pet shop, in the blank tunnels of the subways, she was there, or had just been. She was the presence eternally missed. I could smell her in the sheets. I saw her with her head thrown back, grimacing, even shouting, and her face clear and hot with pleasure.

I missed this most. I missed it dearly, to not have her in my hands, in my arms.

The last thing she said to me in the airport was, "See what the heart brought you?" and kissed me in front of all those people and walked to her plane. What it brought *us,* Claire. What it brought *us.*

She wasn't gone a week before I did something to bury her. She'd given me a leather jacket before she left. It was hers, she said, from her motorcycle days. The brown leather was cracked and so thin in places it turned to powder in my hands. I oiled it. I resewed what I could. Then I wore it around the apartment with nothing on underneath, and tried to feel Claire in it, Claire's body over mine.

But I couldn't feel anything. I couldn't even feel when I touched myself. One night I was crazy with insomnia and got up out of bed and dressed and pulled the jacket on over my clothes. It was too big for me. The sleeves were long and in back it almost covered my ass. I walked to a nearby place I knew where numb-looking people ate hamburgers and drank coffee or beer and listened to what was often terrible music, though quietly off-key, not loud and jarring. I sat in a booth. A young man wearing no jacket, and clothes as carelessly thrown on as mine, asked if he could sit with me. I nodded. We said nothing for a long time, we just listened to the music.

It was a poor imitation of Billie Holiday, but enough like her to remind me how syrupy she used to make me feel. The young man, whose name was Beau, said, "She loved life best when she was singing the blues."

"How do you know?"

"Because aren't we all alike on that one?"

Claire was the little catch in my throat every time I spoke, though the only words I remember saying after we left the booth and walked outside were, "Sometimes I wish

I could be something as simple as hungry, just for the pleasure of getting full again." He nodded. At my apartment he found everything—bowls, herbs, eggs, an egg whisk, the toaster. I still had my jacket on, my hands folded on the table. I turned on the radio and slid through station after station of falsely jubilant discjockese.

"What are you doing that for?" He didn't ask unkindly, but the noise bothered him.

"My friend used to do this."

"I'm surprised it didn't drive you nuts."

I turned it off and we ate. I took off the jacket. I laid my shirt and pants and underwear on what was left of my eggs. I went into the bedroom and laid the jacket underneath me on the floor, and lay on my back and looked up at the cream white ceiling. I pretended I was in a hotel. I pretended this was medicine that would make me well. I heard him washing the dishes and then he came in and took his shirt off and lay it so its shoulder touched mine. He had a hot cheek, I remember. I didn't know who was with me. He did all the work, asking for parts of my body, and he didn't cry out when he came, if he came.

He didn't get up and dress right away. It wasn't like that. I thought he was still inside me a long time after he wasn't. I had a rug burn on my ass and I put on a long shirt to cover it. "Take the jacket," I told him. He was leaving. We stood in the light of the elevator button. "Please take it. It doesn't fit me anymore."

I went home one weekend and the train was filled with ghosts. A different season hung in the windows this time, and there were other changes. Britta was back, but ancient as ever, her stoutness gone. She slid around the kitchen with a metal walker, and the click of its legs on the linoleum was an eerie reminder for all of us in that house.

Rapunzel's grave lay beyond the garden, though the first hole Gus had dug had been out in the corner of the field with the woodchucks. I could imagine Katheryn's voice, "Oh Austin, she *must* be closer to us. We'll plant flowers. Pansies." But all that had succeeded in growing, blanketing the ground with green and curling up around the wooden gravemarker, was poison ivy. Katheryn had a black thumb and Gus wasn't interested in tending to her terriers, dead or alive.

I was home in a different way than I had been before, and this would be the way I would always be home after that. Everything that was important I kept from them; I just needed to be somebody's child. Gus asked about Claire. Katheryn said, "Who's that?" I told them she'd changed jobs and left the city. Gus said, "Well, if you ever need somebody to cut your hair, Fru, I'm here," and shot me one of those looks I'd always loved him for: I hold you, and let you go.

After supper I stood up to clear my place, and Katheryn said, "Frances, have you heard from your old friend Esther?"

"Not in years, Mother."

"Well, I have." She looked triumphant. "I had a letter from her the other day. I've already answered it. She wanted to know all about you, what were your plans, where you lived, whether you were married yet."

Esther! I set my plate on the table again and sat down. "And you told her . . . ?"

"Why, dear, what could I tell her?"

"Who's this?" asked Gus, coming out of the kitchen.

"Oh, you know," said Katheryn. "Esther."

"Esther?"

"Never mind, Austin. Just an old school friend of Frances'. That little colored girl we always liked so much."

"Is this the athletic one?"

"I don't know about athletic," said Katheryn.

"Yes, yes, yes," said my father. "She was the sprinter, wasn't she, Fru? Quick as the devil. Well, what about her?"

"Katheryn's had a letter from her," I said.

"I thought she was your friend."

"Frances' friends can't always keep up with her," said my mother.

Gus shrugged. "I don't know anybody I used to know anymore." He made a cluster of the three wine glasses. We heard him in the kitchen running the faucet full force.

"He soaks the place," said Katheryn. "I don't know why he doesn't leave them for Britta."

We were quiet a moment.

"If you had nothing to tell her, Mother, what did you tell her?"

"Esther? I told her the only thing I knew for certain was that you weren't married." She laughed. "She isn't either. She has a job, some funny job in a zoo or something. Something with animals. It sounded wonderful, and such a wonderful letter; a great girl." She shook her head. "I *have* liked some of your friends, Frances. Why do you always lose touch with the good ones?"

The "zoo or something" was what inspired me, the next day, to write a letter to Esther, and by the end of the week I had an invitation to join her—not zookeeping, but tracking and counting white deer along the California coast. White deer! "After a year of this I'm *lonely*," she had written, "but still as discriminating as ever. You're the only person I know I could get along with who doesn't mind peeing outside in the winter! I've got a one-room place and could make them hire you if you're interested in working for your grade school pal. How are you, anyway?"

But tempting as it was, I couldn't say yes to it.

"I can't leave the pet shop, Mother."

"Oh don't be silly, Frances."

"I have no way of getting out there."

"Is there something the matter with an airplane or bus?"

Gus sat across the room with a book in front of him,

though he could no longer read. I watched him turn the pages from time to time, whenever the old rhythm occurred to him.

"You have to start somewhere," said my mother, and I thought, Start what? and, Why in this way? and, Why am I still unwilling to make Claire's leaving real? "You love animals," Katheryn insisted. "You're good with animals." And as uninformed as it was, her enthusiasm was at least well-intended, and finally contagious. I see it now as the last blooming of maternal instinct, that sleepy bush we'd all thought dead for years. Whatever it was, it knew more about me than I did. It knew I was stifling in the city. It knew I was feeling I didn't have a friend in the world. It knew home was no longer the place for me; that I had courage and humor, and here everything was falling by the way.

So shortly after that I was a traveler, too, following Claire west and knowing I'd never catch her. Knowing I'd get as far as the ocean that separated us, and no farther. I had all I cared to take with me in the trunk and backseat of a Ford Futura that Gus helped me pay for. It was a sturdy old relic, painted a lifeguard bronze with rabbit skin on the dashboard and ninety-nine thousand miles on the odometer. I came to love it for many reasons, but the first and most enduring was its name and make. Stepping into that car was like stepping into a metaphor.

Gus and Katheryn waved me off the first day of October, not knowing exactly who they were waving off, I'm sure. I didn't know either. To kill the miles, I wrote letters to Claire in my head. It was the best I could do because she had left me no address. She wouldn't know exactly where she was until she got there, she told me, and if mail rode the milkboat between islands, which was probably the case, our letters would arrive three weeks after the inspiration that sent them. This wasn't much comfort, and little by little I started addressing the letters to myself instead, turning over each detail like a journalist, as if the most natural thing were to remember it without emotion.

All through that passionate landscape of the South— Virginia, the Carolinas, Georgia, Alabama, Mississippi, and the bayou country of Louisiana—I drove on, stopping often and detouring for days sometimes, but feeling nothing. Not letting myself feel. My journal entries were blunt and businesslike: *Slept next to blue cows outside Charlottesville. Red clay highway, Georgia mountains. Closeup of mattress on front porch, fat boy pulling ticks. Greasy woodsmoke.* No hint of where my heart was, no attempt to reach out to what I saw. Enclosed in glass and metal, I crossed what the miles told me was this country, and except for that split second of bug or butterfly before it crushed itself on my windshield, I filled my eyes with inanimate and inarticulate things.

One night in Alabama, life came right up to my face and still I wouldn't have it. I was driving Interstate 59 with the windows open, feeling the cool wind without liking or hating it. The hills were damp after a rain, and the fog that rose out of the short valleys clung to the car like nylon. Across the interstate the headlights came at me, one slow beaded drop after another, but on my side there was only me in my Futura, hurrying through the darkness.

I thought I'd dozed off and was dreaming, or the fog had whitened and thickened in strange patches on the road. I was in the passing lane, dropping into a valley. Whatever I had seen blew off to the shoulder, and was running the shoulder. Smoke? Ghosts? My own tired eyes imagining? Then suddenly I caught a light in my headlight—a horse's eye. There were at least five of those animals churning down the dirt beside me, spooked by the car. I could have reached out to touch their necks, they were that close. And before I swerved away the closest one ducked so its head was framed by the window, and I thought I could feel its breath on my face as it ran.

I used the adrenaline of that to get me through the

night, though the intimacy of it I pushed away. The nights were best for driving, with their blankness outside the circle of my own headlights. The hours passed. I didn't hurry. A week and then two went by. The hills gave in to the delta, then the high desert of endless Texas, and with the landscape, something changed.

It could have been the hairnet serving me a Coca-Cola at the counter of a Fort Worth Woolworth's—the memory of Britta that this brought me. It could have been many things, the large, squinting people who seemed to throw their lives out in front of them the way New Englanders did not. Or the magpies, the Charlie Chaplins of the bird world, teasing me out of my gloom and emptiness; or the emptiness itself, of place; the space between towns, the barren land that I could only survive by being in contrast to. These were no longer the deep rich woods of home, nor the sweating, peopled byways of the South. I was unknown, unseen except by the few, same-looking strangers who pumped my gas. I finally felt like I connected *them;* that every three hundred miles I brought the hand or scent or oily smudge of one to the other.

My feeling came back to me, that was all. It went out and out, it didn't matter in what direction. One dawn found me high up in the white sand dunes of Alamogordo, no one but me, running, running, kicking in, finding my stride. I feel free! I feel free! I shouted, and tumbled and tucked my head as I rolled in a dozen dizzy somersaults.

Or speeding at ninety, a hundred, practically soaring; pushing the old Futura so it seemed the road wouldn't hold it. And what held me? I came undone from myself at times like that. I was the car, the road, the blunt mesas— all of it. My arms were in the dry creek beds. I was the sky, the sun, endless and giantstepping through reefs of piñon and juniper.

I spent a night in the bleachers in the small town of St. David, Arizona, sleeping little, mostly sitting up watching the high baseball of the stars. Early the next morning I found a motel with day rates where I could take a shower and sit somewhere cool to study my maps. The cicadas were singing, winding themselves into a frenzy in the motel yard. The soft smell of butter and hot cereal slipped through the screen door and met me halfway to the office where a man and a woman were moving inside under a bare light bulb. The light was on, though outside the morning had already turned hot and white, almost too bright to see.

A small sign to the left of the screen door told me in green, day-glo letters that the name of the motel was THE MARILYN. GUESTS EXPECTED. NO GUNS!! To the right of the door a child's P. F. Flyer hung from the arm of a cactus. The cactus leaned dangerously over the motel roof. I knocked, and the man called out, "If you're looking for Mickey, he ain't here yet."

"She ain't looking for Mickey," I heard the woman say. "You want to know why? Just look at that thing she's driving."

The office was their kitchen, and the rooms they rented out were the six cell-sized bedrooms of their house. They slept with their little boy on the patio, or in the kitchen when it rained. Or whenever there was an empty bedroom, they slept there. The morning I arrived, all the bedrooms were empty. The man and the woman had been up all night with flashlights, chasing off town kids impatient for Halloween, who wanted to toilet paper every cactus in The Marilyn's yard.

The man was sitting facing the door when I came in. He was as tall sitting as I was standing. The part of his body that showed above the breakfast table was thin. He was wearing bib overalls and no shirt. A tattoo covered his left shoulder—a dragon that wound down his arm to the elbow. He had a square face that seemed mostly mouth.

The woman sitting next to him was my size, and much younger than him, somewhere between my age and his.

127

Her face was strong and mannish. She had the same walnut tan as he did, and short hair so black it looked blue. She was wearing a pink cotton kimono minus the belt. The word "Darling" hung in gold script from a little gold chain between her breasts. She had tried to tie her short hair up in rollers, and as she drank her coffee her one free hand kept reaching up to shove the rollers back in place, forsaking the kimono. Her breasts, heavy and pale, brushed the tabletop.

The man turned to her. "You look like a astronaut with those things sticking out of your head." He nodded at the open robe. "Cover yourself, Darl. You've got the boobers of a cow."

But at that Darling stretched both hands up and slowly started patting her head, as if it were a cantaloupe she were feeling for ripeness. The robe flapped open. She lowered her arms and the kimono fell down from her shoulders.

"You hungry?" she asked me. I told her I was.

"She should have been a actress," said the man, nodding at Darling.

We ate together, hot cereal on a plate with butter and syrup poured over it. We ate fast, without talking, and when we were done we still didn't talk. I listened to the cicadas and the soft *puh-puh* of bugs battering the screen. Darl pinched her robe together and reached up to switch off the light that dangled above us on a frayed cord. But before she switched it off, she held the light bulb at an angle so it lit up the man's lap. "See that? An ice truck got him. Fuckers didn't pay a cent," she said.

Both the man's legs ended above the knee. His overalls were cut off and pinned there, I'll never forget, with four big silver safety pins that seemed too bright for that room.

"Tell her how they itch, Papa."

The man said nothing. Suddenly he pulled the table-

128

cloth into his lap, and plates and glasses rolled into his lap, then fell to the floor and shattered. Now I could see that the chair he sat in was a wheelchair. Darling shone the light at his head and he hid his face behind the lifted edge of the tablecloth. He was shaking, and his hands were shaking. She said, "Tell her how you sit up sometimes and scratch the air, and they quit itching."

I heard a sound like a sob behind me as I hurried through the yard. The hot butter and syrup had spread through me so I felt my veins were made of it. There was a cat squatting on a cracked toilet bowl, and a tree in the yard with mitten-shaped leaves whose shade I wanted to gather to me as I ran.

I drove north and west, and took the roads less traveled by the rest of the way to California. I counted fifty shades of brown one evening just before sunset, my hour of estrangement in the desert. The sky that day had been pestered with vultures and hawks, and suddenly I felt the turning season, autumn's sobriety in those wings you could see through, wheeling in circles. And as if that weren't warning enough to keep going, to keep leaning, mind, heart and body toward the ocean, I had a vision, as real in the rearview as the manmade lake that stretched out in front of me for miles, Lake Powell, and the dammed Colorado, where I'd come to see a few sea gulls before the long haul across Utah and Nevada. I had parked at the end of a narrow dirt road in a cluster of trailers where Page, Arizona, thinned out and lost itself again to the deserted plateau. One of the trailers was brown, two were pink, one was turquoise. My eyes followed the sea gulls for a while then drifted up to the rearview. I saw him outside the turquoise, an old man in a chair, taking in the sun under a full clothesline of women's underwear. He had his hands up, his pale arms, and he was touching the cups of the bras like they were the first snow of the year just fallen.

1

When I told Esther I loved women she was overjoyed, though if she had kicked me out I would have been no more surprised. The last time I'd seen her was the day seventh grade ended, and she was punishing a classmate by banging the poor girl's head against a boulder in Carl Schurz Park.

Esther was a small, athletic black woman who hated, as much as I did, the private school we went to in New York. If it hadn't had one of the best softball teams in the city, we might really have run away together, instead of just dreaming about it. Through most of sixth grade we were inseparable, and would spend our afternoons at Esther's house, trying to decipher the mysterious codes of the bus schedules we discovered in the top drawer of her father's dresser. Only years later, after Claire's stories about her own family, did I wonder at that man who hoarded dreams of escape and adventure under the neat piles of his underwear and rolled-up socks. His passion was for the Pacific Northwest, so this had to be the destination we dreamt about, too, though I'm sure the places that caught our imaginations were different from the ones that caught his. Humptulips, Washington, or Sweet Home, Oregon. These were the strange syllables that took up our eleven-year-old days.

Esther's family finally did move away, the next year, to Baltimore and then St. Louis, but before that we discovered something more exotic than travel to fill our wishful afternoons. This was softball. My friend played catcher, I played pitcher, and each of us took on the postures and language of those positions as if we were born for them. She loved catcher for the same reason I hated it: the fifty-fifty chance of ending up with the ball in your glove. That, for me, was too arbitrary, too unsettling, too much like the rest of puberty. When I pitched, I could put the ball exactly where I wanted it.

I loved having Esther on the receiving end of my curve or change-up, and I really could throw curves and change-ups. We were sophisticated. We had a coach who believed in us. She called Esther, Roy Campanella Jr., and let her lug around the equipment, forty pounds of bats and bases any one of us would have happily shouldered. Her name was Miss Bing, "like bing cherries." She had a Moe, of the Three Stooges, haircut, red hair, and a vendetta against the sun. We practiced three afternoons a week on Randall's Island, and Bing always wore what looked like white pajamas and a sailor hat and carried a black umbrella. For some reason we weren't embarrassed by her getup, possibly because she'd taken the opportunity to show us what became of her without it.

I remember a tight, sweaty circle of girls around her one afternoon, big and little twelve-year-old bodies reeking of underarms and neatsfoot oil, while Miss Bing slowly, dramatically, offered us her arm. Out and out she stretched it, and held it where each one of us could take it in. "This," she said, "is the result of a sleeveless shirt and having forgotten my umbrella." The arm, which only hours before had been evenly pale, was now dotted with hundreds of freckles. One of us shamefully said, "Ew," and some other joker: "It looks like sticky flypaper!" That, I believe, was Maggie Britton, shortstop, whom Esther forgave only after cracking her head against a rock that last day of school.

Now, almost twelve years later, I told my friend there was something I still loved about the smell of close spaces where athletes had just spent some time. Like squash courts or certain corners of locker rooms. I woke to this smell every morning, and to the sight of Esther peeling off sweatpants and a sweatshirt after one of her long, dawn runs.

Eventually we ran together at a pace where Esther could comfortably talk and I could breathe, though barely. My chest burned, my legs burned. I felt how long my body had been inside, in a city. But the hour was beautiful, and I let the watery sun or the fog coax me out into a rhythm of legs and arms that became my own. We ran the half mile of woods between the cabin where we lived and the bluffs that dropped steeply into the ocean. We ran the bluffs north on a trail that cut right along the top of the cliff, and sometimes while Esther went out an extra mile, I stood at the edge and looked two hundred feet down into the spume of the Pacific.

It was a boyish ocean, a kind of young lover to the matronly Atlantic; green in the calm, but with a wild surf on storm days. I once asked Esther if there was anything in the world she was afraid of, and she answered, "That ocean."

"Why?"

"Because of what you can't see."

On one of our longer runs she stopped with me in a place where I'd stopped and stood and looked down a dozen times before, and she pointed at something just emerging in the ebbing tide: the bodies of sheep, broken on the rocks below us. I counted forty. Another day I came back at a lower tide and counted forty more. They had been there some time. They were bones and very little flesh, with limbs flung up wherever the sea had dragged them, and the sea foam circling them like wool. The next time I came, some of the bones had slipped down between the rocks. Others, the snapped thigh bones that had pointed skyward, had been rolled flat by the waves.

Esther had a kayak, and when we weren't running or working, we took turns paddling out in it and surfing home. Or we played in the woods, real woods of fallen leaves and soft, boggy places that brought New Jersey to me. My friend knew just where the white deer, or Tule elk as they were called, were most likely to be, and when we found them, counted them and recorded time and place, our work was over and the day was ours to play in. Esther was better at play than I was, so I let her lead me from one thing to the next. She invented games with strange names, like Mud-Spud-And-Get-Out-Of-Here and Rin-Tin Roofball—each a kind of sawed-off version of softball. We pitched horseshoes, we built a swing, and one incredible day we built a tree fort big enough for both of us to sleep in, which we did whenever the cabin's one room started to seem too familiar.

"A tree fort, Esther! We're almost twenty-four years old!"

"It's a shame about you, Franny," she said, letting loose with the hammer. "You had to wait this long to build a tree fort, poor baby!"

Her only rule to live by was: If it gets old, change it. Which is why she was always a surprise to me. She surprised me the day I first saw her with the Tule elk. She had run ahead of me on the dirt road, and they came tiptoeing out of the oaks, about ten of them, sniffing the wind that came from behind them. So they had no warning of us. I stopped as soon as I saw them. She crouched down. They were hurrying to cross the road and some were so close to her, my side of her, that the herd almost parted around her as if she were a rock in the stream. But at the last minute they spooked and leapt in all directions. They looked at first like they were leaping out of her hair. She was suddenly the dark center of all this white life, and a column of sun through the oaks perfected it.

Later, her dark body against the white of sheets, not deer, surprised me. It was bound to happen. She was boiling over that day. All morning she had sung Billie Holiday through the woods at the top of her voice, a much closer rendering of the real thing than the last Billie Holiday I'd heard. We came home for lunch but neither of us wanted to eat. We took all our clothes off and lay on the double bed we'd shared since the night I arrived.

We were always affectionate. Esther had an exuberance of body that usually goes when childhood goes. I often woke up in the middle of the night to find she'd fallen asleep holding my hand. But this, this time, was the fire in her, not the little girl. She was suddenly above me in the bed, at the top of what seemed like a push-up. Dear, athletic Esther. I felt her wrists trapping my shoulders. She held herself up on arms that didn't shake, I noticed, though it seemed she hung over me for a very long time.

"Franny, you love me now like you've loved some other women," was all she said—not a question, a very clear command. When I thought of those "other women," of course there was only one. I remembered it was three months to the day that Claire had left, and I guess I looked at it then as my going away gift to us both.

Oh, my gift to Esther, too, and hers to me. All that sweet, comfortable skin again and no one in a hurry to go anywhere. I'd never had such playful sex before. We laughed at the oddness of our lives coming around again to where they began, with Esther on the receiving end of my giving, even squatting or kneeling in front of me just as she had behind homeplate. And when she touched me I remembered it all, forgot it all, then lay quietly next to her, breathing deeply, and remembered it all again. Women were made of something that day. We were made of something.

We made love often after that. It was always friendly, gratifying sex. We worked and lived together well, and we became each other's favorite companion. She was still more adventurous than I was, and seemed to attract luck in an uncanny, hilarious way. Once she took me into Berkeley to a bodybuilders' competition, and when we arrived, to our surprise, all those beautiful torsos belonged to women! Long blondes, short brunettes, even one woman with a shaved head! But all with oiled and gleaming skin, dressed in tiny bikinis and flexing muscles I never knew we had.

Another time we drove down to San Francisco for something Esther had seen advertised as a Witches' Ball. It took place in the third- or fourth-string ballroom of the Marriott Hotel, and when we arrived, the small room was wall-to-wall women. Women in blue jeans, women in tuxedoes. Eerie, masked women—though no broomsticks—and wholesome country types whom Esther called "the wholegrain gypsies." We split up at the door. This was Esther's idea and she was lovely that night in loose, pastel clothes, cornrowed hair. The whole room could have been dancing. It was impossible to tell who was and who wasn't. I was wearing a wide-brimmed hat which alternately cut me off from everyone and brought me too much attention. In a moment when I was feeling cut off I asked someone who looked like a swimmer to dance. She said, "Why not?" which was more an "I've got nothing else to do," but at the time I was flooded with gratitude, and all I could say was, "Really?"

At some point that evening I looked across the room and there was Esther behind a cluster of silver and black balloons that reminded me of caviar, adoring a short blond woman who looked quite a lot like me. They were deep kissing in whatever way it was about Esther that made each thing she did have its absolute place in her whole life. And if you were with her it had its place in yours too. And even if you were just watching, you felt it. I'd half expected to be angry or jealous, but here it was, a solid beam of love, from me to her and from her to me. A circle of it, taking in the short blond woman and everyone else in the room. Like an old game of catch. Much larger than our going to bed together.

What was it, Claire? To love one woman is to love all women? Yes! I was alone that night and succeeded in dancing with whomever I wanted—even with the two barmaids who would have looked more comfortable in a bowling alley. I was sure they were old closets and would go home and tell Harold and Bill about what they saw. But bless them, they taught me how to Charleston! And on the front kick each sent a shoe flying over the heads of the crowd. When it was over we all had that look of having just finished the richest food.

After that night, whenever I came away from the woods and into a crowd or a city, I was aware, always as if for the first time, that the world was populated by women. For a year before that, the world had been populated only by Claire. But now I saw them everywhere. Esther did too, though I suspect she always had. We were amused and amazed by bodies, faces, eyes that did or didn't meet; shoes, clothes, hairstyles: disguises! Or the infrequent naked limb, out of place and out of season in the city. Too bad! Women hung on corners, like prostitutes but not—simply waiting for a light to change. They were visible in windows, in cars, driving taxis, some of them; others lugging packages or children, or both. They were like us more than they weren't like us, or as Esther said, even the ones who weren't like us were like us, "And thank god for that!"

When we weren't gawking we were in the woods, together or apart, silent sometimes for days. Esther taught me how to run her chain saw, and we got in enough wood to keep the cabin warm all winter. The ocean wind was chill and relentless. By Thanksgiving it stung our faces to stand out in it on the trail along the bluffs. The Tule elk hid, but somebody still kept sheep, and I liked to use their far bodies as destinations whenever I ran or walked.

Esther's Christmas present to me arrived in the form of a question one morning after breakfast. "Franny," she asked, "have you ever seen your cervix?"

"Dear god, Esther, I'd have to be a contortionist, wouldn't I? Have you?"

"Ha!" she laughed. "Just what I hoped. Come away with me for an hour, will you? Grab a sweater and put that morbid junk away."

That "morbid junk" was Dostoevsky's *Crime and Punishment,* which I finally found myself old enough to read. Esther's opinion of literature had always been different than mine. In seventh grade, when the rest of us were falling in love with Odysseus, reading *The Odyssey* as if it were hot pornography, she kept the real stuff in the back of her desk—*Fanny Hill, Candy, The Wayward Girl.* She tucked the jacket of *The Odyssey* around each one as she brought it out, and our teacher believed her appetite for Homer was enormous.

We drove to Karen's house. Karen was a distant neighbor and a friend of Esther's who worked as a midwife in the community where we lived. She was expecting us. She'd spread a peach-colored blanket on the kitchen table—no straps, no stirrups, no awesome-looking equipment. She used only a speculum, a flashlight and a small pocket mirror. "There you go," she said, angling the mirror so I could see what looked so much like a nose up inside me I half expected the rest of the face to show itself while I watched.

Once before, snorkeling in a Massachusetts cove, I had felt what I felt that day, legs spread, on Karen's table.

That time my awe had been in reaction to a pretty colored fish that swam by me at arm's distance—the first time I'd seen a fish at home, underwater, where it belonged. And though its colors dazzled me and the way it swam was a dance, my awe had little to do with that. It was the awe of entering another world for the first time. Water had always meant the water's surface to me, and a fish was something stretching its gills in a tackle bag. But down there it was so much brighter! so much better! I thought, Such a well-kept secret!

And this too! There I was, big-eyed, staring up the canal of my vagina to the tip of the womb—*my* womb! I don't think I'd ever used the word until that day, but then I couldn't stop saying it. *Womb . . . womb . . . womb. . . .* It began to sound like baby talk for "room," which suddenly seemed no coincidence.

Karen held the mirror while I rocked this way and that in front of it, trying to see as much of myself as there was to see. "My god, you're beautiful," I said to myself, and out loud. And I realized I might have been talking, for the first time, to the me of me.

That was the season's grand event, and for a couple of months afterward the winter seemed immovable—a steady, dark, starless presence that finally yielded something memorable around the time of my birthday. I had gone alone into Berkeley, to a small bookshop where paperbacks were practically giveaways and a couple of stuffed chairs filled a space in front of the window. I usually went in a few times a month and spent the whole day there, reading and watching people who now, in my relative isolation, tended to resemble all the living ghosts of my life. As if some part of everyone I'd ever known was present in these strangers. A nose might remind me of Gus, or a mannerism of Katheryn. Probably I was just more attuned to the human ingredient we all shared, because those days I saw so many more trees than people.

This time I was half asleep in one of the chairs with my legs tucked under me like a wing, and I don't remember what book open in my lap. I had been thinking of Claire that week, and that day in particular the musty-sweet smell of the bookstore, or possibly some old scent left in the pages I was reading, brought her back to me. Not painfully. Calmly. Like I was ready for her again. The man in the chair next to me had just sat down, I remember, and when he turned to look at me, to see who his company was, or what I was reading, there was Claire. She was in his face, in his features and expression. It was the first face since hers that I hadn't been able to look away from. It gave off a heat, an intensity I could feel in the rush of color to my cheeks and forehead.

I think he said, "Oh, excuse me." I must have looked frightened or feverish. Then of his own he got up and moved away. If I had turned around I might have seen that he walked as Claire walked, or I might have seen him again as the absolute stranger he was, if he was.

The end of that day came with a letter, more of a whole chapter, really. Twenty handwritten pages stuffed in a manila envelope, from Claire. I knew it when I drove up to the cabin after dark, and in the light of the headlights saw the lid of our hanging mailbox propped open, the manila showing. I came right up to it and saw the stamps first, the postmarked face of some political general in triplicate, and one of a waterfall behind reclining, tropical girls. Hello, Claire, I thought. What brings you here? And suddenly I remembered the ocean; how all these months we had shared it and I had never even thought of that. She could have sent a message in a bottle! The Japanese Current was with us, wasn't it?

I didn't want to tear it open. I had a wild idea to take it down and throw it in the waves; wait for it to wash in again; see if it really belonged there in my hands. But instead I put my nose to it, then laughed to think how long it had been out of *her* hands. It should smell more of steamers and breadfruit and chickens, and possibly the last airport it had passed through to get here.

I didn't save it until morning as I thought I might. Esther was gone for a couple of days and the cabin was a perfect place to stay awake in. I built up the fire. I set a kerosene lamp on the table beside me. It was one of those rare nights, so still and cold you could hear the stars crack, or imagine it. And the other sound was the ocean, a faint booming that made me feel so much in the presence of another person that I got up and lit a second lamp in the window, and only then began to read.

8

February 7th
Ponape

Dear, sweet Franny,

So long since I've called you by name! I am hoping
this will arrive in time for your birthday and will hold
enough to make up for the crate of flowers I was going to
send you. It was one of those crates they use to send co-
conuts in and I lugged it to the mailing station only to be
told that flowers can't travel. For some reason they won't
let them off the islands. But the blooms here are so gorgeous, I just wanted you to have some of them, too, going
through your drab winter. An odd thing is that on Ponape
the men, not the women, wear the flowers. They love to
dress themselves in the blossoms and turn heads wherever
they go, their fragrance wafting through the streets and
even in the marketplace that smells (stinks!) of so many

other things. I half believe it was sheer possessiveness that made the man at the mailing station tell me my flowers couldn't get to you. But I hope they come close, dear Franny. They're slowly rotting in their box, and I'm leaning back against the box they're rotting in. Their smell—each bloom different—reached a kind of crescendo about an hour ago that woke me from my sleep. I felt I was drowning in it. Now they are less and less each minute and before I began this letter to you I said goodbye to them.

My only close friend here was born the day after you, though sixteen years earlier, which brings him up to ten years old (!), finally, this year. Funny the things we never talked about, though it seems we talked incessantly for all those months. I've started keeping a notebook of all I would have said to you and hopefully will have the chance to say to you someday. It begins: "Ask Franny her feelings about luck. For instance, does it strike her as lucky or unlucky to have been born on February 28th, in a Leap Year?" Shakespeare, my friend here, has become a kind of popular hero due to the infrequency of his birthday. Everyone loves an oddball, he says. But more about him later.

Katheryn sent me your California address, no questions asked. What are you onto, Franny? In her note to me your mother seemed to think you'd gone mad, living like Thoreau somewhere—no heat, no plumbing! Reading and writing by candlelight. Leading the monk's life was what she meant, though she didn't say it. I understand perfectly, though I can't help wonder who, if anyone, is making your time there worthwhile. Or maybe that's the job of the place, which I've only heard is lovely. Good for you! whatever you have, whatever you're doing, my friend.

It's so hard to speak to you in this moment without sounding insincere. It's so hard to break a silence; to begin again well when we didn't end well. But stay with me, Franny. I'm trying, I'm trying, I'm trying to break into my heart—that stubborn meat. Like a burglar . . .

In the room where I'm writing there are blue shades and a lazy overhead fan that squeaks for lack of oil. It reminds me of the nighthawk that hung above our heads by the docks our last evening together. The one I called an albatross, and then you laughed—I loved that laugh. The best part of the day is now, the twilit hour at the end of the night when you have to pull the sheet over you or you're uncomfortably cool. Before and after that it's too hot to sleep, but here's this beautiful little ceasefire that you want to be awake for, to relish it. Though asleep, it gives you a sleep without dreams, one peace-filled hour. It's the hour when the ashram comes alive, though it's a life you can neither hear nor see. I can feel it now as I write.

There are twelve of us "devotees" at the moment, though the number varies. In the short time I've been here we've been down to four and had as many as twenty-four. Each of us has a private "cell," which is a bare, whitewashed room with shades and a fan. There is a mat on the floor for sleeping, and one sheet. The ashram provides each of us with a Bible, a Bhagavad Gita and the Tibetan Book of the Dead. This adds a sort of eclectic, motel touch to the place that would make old Gideon roll over in his grave, I'm sure! My trunk, carted around by both of us that last day in the city, dropped out of the picture almost the minute I got here. I just don't need *things*. Grandmama's Buddha I've kept with me, but the clothes and books went to an orphanage across the island. It was strange and beautiful on my last visit there to see in the streets a young boy I thought I knew from somewhere, though how could I have known him? a ten or twelve-year-old Micronesian boy, only to realize it was the clothes, not the person I recognized. He was wearing my lavender shirt—your favorite, and though the sleeves hung on him and he didn't half fill the shoulders, he was gorgeous in it. I told him so, or tried to in his language. It was meant for dark skin or a deep tan after all. As for the books, I laugh whenever I think of all those orphans pulling Beowulf from the shelf, or May Sarton's poetry. I wish I'd had the foresight to bring the Oz books, and though I'm happy you have it (with the cover loved off!), The Velveteen Rabbit.

From three in the morning (it's only a little after that now) until six, we meditate. Breakfast after that and then the business of the day. Most of us here have some kind of job on the island, or on one of the atolls. We're not paid for it. We're fed and sheltered by the ashram, and what would we do with the money? It's thought of as service, just as the meditation is; just as our entire life will someday be. My job varies more than anyone else's because I've discovered I'm unskilled in every way! No one here needs a semi-professional decorator, which is all the museum job really came down to. But I like this, building a wall one week and sewing up a boy's foot the next. There's an Australian woman here, Miranda, who's a doctor, and when I work with her I feel her utter devotion to the lives of others.

There are so many here, Franny, who are far more advanced than me. I'm still trying to clear a direct line between what's in me—the real me—and what comes out of me. I can't tell you what the real me is like, but I can recognize it (I think you always could too). When there's no distance between my face or my words, and who I am, that's it. It feels perfect. I feel comfortable. I don't plan it or think about it, or if I do, that's never when it happens. I don't earn it. It's what the Christians call "grace," what poets call "the Muse." I'm just trying to learn to be grateful for the moments when I'm in it. That's odd, isn't it, because really it's in me—*all the time, waiting.* It's what's left after the costume comes off, when I've shrunk my ego down to nothing and all my illusions of being what I'm not are gone.

After work we come together for a meal, usually silent, and then a three-hour meditation before bed. We are a quiet bunch, but our function here together isn't social. We are all denominations, from all over the world, but spend little time learning more about each other's backgrounds or longings, as those just seem part of the costume we're trying to throw off. For example, Roger and Miranda have been here longer than I have, and though we are friends in a deep way, we don't seem to know (or care!) how to build the kind of relationships that people build in the world. So I feel very solitary now, though not a bit lonely. Though I do wonder how well I'll stand up to the rest of the world when I come back to it. Both Miranda and Roger left the ashram before they were strong enough— Roger to London, Miranda to Connecticut—and both ended up back in their cells again after only a year. (Sounds like dear Lydia's stories about every convict's addiction to prison!) But when I see them now I think, my god, they're two of the soundest, most selfless human beings I'll ever meet— but they're still here! I only hope and pray what seems true isn't true, Fran: That there's no place for that kind of giving, strength and selflessness out there where we live.

I've been told that in a year and a half I won't be ready to come home, so I've committed myself to two more years after that at the ashram. Why am I reminded, in telling you this, of the time you hauled home that sack of fresh figs from the Greek deli? God, I remember how plump and what a sweet purple they were! There must have been fifty in the bag and you sat in the window with a knife across your knees, halving them and folding back the edges of each half as you sucked out the little pink-seeded heart. After ten of them you looked like a woman with a bruised mouth. Your lips were pink and swollen. You said, "Claire, I adore you," and maybe you did. "If you love me, come make yourself sick on figs."

You were unstoppable. I didn't believe a person could get drunk on them, but you were drunk on them. I might have eaten one; the rest were yours. You were through them in half an hour and then you were sick all afternoon in my apartment, sick all that night.

It's possible to love what may hurt you, Franny; in fact it seems the best way to live—true fearlessness. You, my sweet one, were truly fearless sitting up there gobbling little purple and green explosives, then resting, I remember, with one hand over your eyes, the other over your belly, waiting for the bombs to go off. I hope I'm fearless, sitting still in the quiet of this haven, growing more and more solitary; testing myself at that edge where loneliness has always come in in the past. I'm so removed from carnal love, passion, exuberance, despair. I may be hurting myself—even killing myself, or truly coming to life, I don't know which. My surroundings may be the best thing in the world for me, or all wrong. And I won't come home until I've eaten down to the bottom of the bag and made myself sick—or cured myself.

February 9th

Yesterday was too busy to write. Shakespeare's son is an epileptic, and yesterday he had a series of seizures that frightened the family so badly they brought him in to the clinic by boat. Miranda and I were loaded down with work. She was in one room delivering triplets and had me in the other giving vaccinations. What a universe! When Shakespeare and company arrived (he, his wife and three handsome sons), there was nothing to do but call off the vaccinations and do what I could to settle little Iago's fit—and pray for a quick delivery in the next room. But it wasn't quick, and except for a few moments of Miranda's presence which calmed everyone, I had to do for the poor little kid myself. Which meant mainly just clearing away everything in the room that he could cut or bruise himself on, and letting him fling his body around until he wore himself out, wore down the demon in him. This seems such a beautiful solution, now that I think of it. The Tao of medicine.

It lasted about ten minutes and ended with Iago literally falling, already asleep, into my lap. Shakespeare's payment, though none is asked, has always been to take me fishing. So he'll come today to the ashram after breakfast, and together we'll go out.

He's an enormous black man, darker than most of the islanders and one of the largest human beings I've ever seen. He has bright blue eyes (from his Portuguese mother) and a long, loose face. His hands are about the size of my head (actually closer to your head, which I remember is a little smaller than mine). His big body seems bigger for being fat and soft, though "in his prime" he was impressive enough. His wife showed me a picture of them on their wedding day, and Shakespeare's a boulder pile of muscles, near bursting out of his cotton suit. His sons are the most important thing in the world to him, and one of them, Prospero, shares a Leap Year birthday with his father. This is how I discovered that there isn't a word in their language for "coincidence," or even any real concept of it. In fact here, whatever distinguishes a man from the rest, he expects to pass on to his son. So Prospero has inherited the birthday and Iago and Brutus have inherited Shakespeare's size. You can already see them swimming in their bodies, which are giant-stepping out of boyhood though the boys are still very young.

Shakespeare is one of the few adults in his village who has an education, and he speaks English more fluently than I do—and more fluidly! My god, he turns it into a song! There wasn't an ashram nor an ashram school here when he was growing up, but he tells me his mother fought his father bitterly to keep him out of the boats every morning so she could teach him at home. And the same battle is still going on in the islands, though women like Shakespeare's mother are rare. Most kids are put to work as soon as they can walk, as soon as they're weaned and become another mouth to feed. Little three- and four-year-old boys are sent out after fish, or sent to mend nets all day (and an older sister sent with them to see that they don't drown, though she herself can't swim). Sometimes Prospero, Brutus and Iago are the only kids in school for weeks. They are smart. Their English is already good and Roger has had fun reading them the plays they still think their father wrote, in which each of them is the villain or hero. Even their own death they take with a certain amount of pride. Brutus stood up in the classroom when the time came to act it out and plunged half an inch of pencil into his chest! (By luck he was wearing a shirt that day.)

When I go fishing with Shakespeare, I see something in it for him that wouldn't be there if he'd grown up with it as his work. The same is in it for me. He brings two bottles of homemade beer. I pack sandwiches from the ashram. The water is an ice-blue color before the wind darkens it. All the working fishermen have gone out hours ago. We have the whole, silent cove to ourselves, and Shakespeare always points out his shack at the end of the peninsula as we pass it. Sometimes his wife, whose name I don't know, is out hanging up the pants and shirts and sheets—all a blinding white—and recognizing the skiff, she waves. Or if both arms are taken, she cocks her head. Always Shakespeare laughs. If they haven't quarreled that morning, he blows her a kiss with both hands. He has a big love, like you do; like I don't yet, and may never, though I know there can be nothing without it. No god, no music, no real you or me. No real hope, whatever that means. I love him for his love, as I love you for yours. It's a love shown, unlike Miranda's which is a love sent inward, to be the strength and ground for everything she does. Your love, and this man's, is the bloom.

I don't think it matters whether it goes to ground or

flower, if it's a big enough love, that's all that matters. I'm close to Shakespeare in a way I could never be close to Miranda or anyone else at the ashram, though I care deeply for them. Maybe I make them too extraordinary, too saintly, and scare myself away. But to the people of the island, Shakespeare's a sort of saint, which here means that he does well what he does. He speaks well, and gets drunk well. He has a fine, handsome family whom he doesn't neglect, and a job of great responsibility (he's the local grocer). He's often called upon to settle disputes. In emergencies he has performed marriages. He so entangles himself in the ordinary that his saintliness is utterly human. Or it's his humanness that's saintly. Well now, why don't I feel the same is true of all of us here at the ashram as we try to connect ourselves to the simple, everyday tasks? As we try to be lighter? As we try to silence the voices that chatter and judge incessantly? The difference may be that someone like Shakespeare hasn't had to try, though I don't know. His life just comes naturally to him. (He will laugh today when I tell him this!)

Later. After evening meditation. I love coming back to this, giving this time to you, though I know it's only stories still and there are endless layers to get through before I'm with you, my bare self. I caught a shark for you this morning, dear Franny. I fought it in for over an hour, an enormous five-foot beauty that finally seemed to climb out of the sea of its own after we had utterly exhausted each other. I wouldn't have been able to hold on much longer if it hadn't surrendered—so we were equals. Shakespeare was just beaming. We had spent much too long talking abstractly about effort, a continuation of some of my earlier thoughts to you. He doesn't understand how anyone, by effort, could come closer to living the life they're already living, and I must say, put this way it made me feel foolish. But then the fish jumped up and saved us with a tug on my line I thought might take my arm off. Shakespeare told me I'd caught the island and I suddenly wanted to believe him. I was terrified, holding who knew what configuration of flesh on a hook way down there where I couldn't see it. I imagined many things. I imagined the devil with horns (this after glimpsing that devil's tail swipe the water's surface halfway through the battle). If Shakespeare hadn't been there I would have cut the line or chucked the rod in the sea to be done with it. I'd never hooked anything so alive before. Just snapper and Moorish idols that seemed like dime store fish, and once as a very little girl in Canada with my father, some rainbow trout.

It was so stinking hot and bright out there the sweat was pouring off me. Shakespeare rigged some shade with the spare oars and a blanket, but nothing was steady enough and the little tent collapsed. He doused me with buckets of sea water (I can invoke a Proustian moment now, hours later, by licking the salt off my arm). At the end he stood behind me, chin on my shoulder and his arms around my waist in a tight bear hug to keep me upright and in the boat. I was gasping—beautifully, Franny, like the fish in me was responding to its other on the end of the line. Shakespeare kept saying, "Thot's you lova! You tangling with you lova! Now hold him tight, hold him tight! Think like he think, roll with him! Be in a sexy way with thot fish, Claire, or you lose him! You got to know him. Now breathe when he breathe. He's running now! Let it out, let it out! You run with him!"

So finally, with my eyes closed, I tried to love the fish. And I was surprised. This was much easier than being afraid of it. By the time we dragged it into the boat I knew the beast's heart; I knew its lungs as well as my own, and how its chest must be aching now for water as mine did for air. I also knew we were on opposite ends of everything. It was going down, I was rising. Shakespeare slipped the boat hook through its gills. I pulled on the tail. It was rough as a man's cheek and easy to hold on to, but so heavy. Luckily the shark had lost its will and wanted to be with us, otherwise we would have had to abandon it there or tow it home with its friends and brothers feeding on it all the way in. Usually you have to break the skull with a club (all the fishermen here carry American-made baseball bats for just that purpose), but Leviathan lay on the narrow deck as if she were asleep. We tied ropes over and around her. She started to shrink in the sun.

We carried her back to Shakespeare's beach and his wife and boys came down with, of all things, a camera! One of those ancient Polaroids. I so wanted to lie in the sand and wrap my arms around my fish instead of standing up next to it in the classic, touristy pose! So we did it that way. In the photograph, Shark looks so docile, so human, lying next to me. We could be shipwrecked together. She was rough as her tail all over except in a long triangle at her throat. The skin was smooth and white there. The rest of her was blue. She frightened me again at the end when my head was close to hers and her eyes narrowed and she gave out a final gust of breath. She looked evil. Shakespeare said, "There go the soul." We left his sons hacking her apart with axes—something I didn't turn around to see, but couldn't help hearing before it was all drowned by the motor's noise. I'm happy. That will be meat for that family for a week.

I must get this off to you or never expect it to arrive by the 28th. Still, I haven't said enough. I feel my own inadequacy in not being able to tell you what's truly in me. I am trying to get at this through meditation. I am trying to let each moment be a window into infinity; to perceive the infinite in each object or gesture. So no grandness is required, but even the smallest thing is part of a grandness. You. Me. The throat of a shark. In this light (this way of seeing), I know I have nothing to be afraid of. The actual, physical light of one candle throws a shadow across the wall, and I can understand it as a creeping, terrifying monster, or my hand scribbling as fast as it can to include all my heart, now open, in this letter. In my good moments, in my moments of grace, I reach here. What concentration it requires! What giving up! Can you ever forgive me for not loving you enough? For not *knowing* you enough?

I'm left alone now in this dead still of night with my answer to that miles and days away across the ocean. This sitting here in silence, aware of the taste and shape and poignancy of each moment that goes by, this is my love for you. *Tell her. You still have not told her. Before you back away and cover yourself again, for god's sake tell her:* I love you, Franny. Dear soul, I do love you.

Many Oms I send you on this starry night, lacking even the sound of the ocean. Be whole. Be well. Your Claire.

9

I here. She had said it. She
was struggling still, my friend, to let herself love me, and
for this I could love her all the more. Or hate her for
having to struggle, this grown woman. Or pity her for
being born under a stubborn star. But for a good long
time after reading that letter, my mind was just a glorious
blank. I had a strange impulse to warm my hands, though
the fire had the room almost too hot. I laced my fingers
around the globe of the lamp without touching the glass.
Dark, winged monsters threw themselves up on the cabin
walls.

I might have sat an hour. I thought I heard rain and
then the faint distress of roosters crowing far away in the
night. But it was only the gulls calling, and the rain was a
light, wet snow that had come up suddenly between where
I stood by the window looking out at it, and the stars. I
put on my hat and jacket and walked to the bluffs. I came

back to the cabin, undressed, and dressed again in long underwear and Esther's rubber wet suit. The suit covered everything but my hands, feet and head, and walking outside again with the snow coming down on me, I felt tarred and feathered.

I went the long way around to the beach where Esther kept the kayak. The paddle was shoved inside it but the spray-skirt had blown away or was buried somewhere in the sand. That meant I would have no way of keeping the ocean out of the boat, and if I went over I would be thrown out instead of rolling with the kayak as Esther had taught me to do.

"The point is to wear the boat," she had told me, "to make the boat and paddle extensions of your body. When you've got that you'll be able to feel yourself becoming the ocean. You move as it moves. You roll with it. That's the only way to stay upright."

But tonight it didn't matter. The waves' motion made me impatient to be out in them, and inside the wet suit I was so sweaty the thought of a lapful of water seemed fine to me. As I bent over to shoulder the little fiberglass kayak I was filled with love of the familiar effort bound up in physical endeavor. That tangible crimp at the junction of neck and shoulder that relieved itself the moment I set the kayak down. It was a light boat, weighing less than thirty pounds, but twelve feet long and awkward to carry those fifty yards to the water. I laid it in the damp sand and went back for the paddle. It was only then that I realized what a storm this suddenly was. The snow had become dense like a thick fog and I had to follow my own footprints back to find the paddle.

Only my bare feet knew how cold it was, and my hands, and the stripe of my face below my hat and above the collar of the wet suit. I walked a few yards out into the sea, pushing the boat lightly ahead of me with one hand and floating the paddle beside me with the other. The water was mid-thigh. My feet were numbly planted in what seemed like another country, and between me and this country ran the lifeline of my legs. I had this crazy urge to worship something, to drop to my knees that were hidden below the water and worship all the muscles of my body. It had been weeks since I'd called upon my physical self, and now this made even the smallest movement a wonder to me. I felt powerful. I could feel the going and coming of the ocean, hard and persuasive between my thighs, and seconds later hear those same waves flopping on the beach. I couldn't see the beach behind me for the snow. I was encircled. I was an island of flesh and rubber and one wool hat, half woman, half water. An aquataur.

I lifted one leg into the boat, leaned across it, and lifted in the rest of my body. Or rather, the legs lifted themselves and my torso leaned to balance without being told to. I was living in my senses. The wisdom of the body ran with me. I tried a few unwilling strokes with the paddle and knew I'd have to do better than that to leave the beach at all.

I spent the first minutes just trying to keep from going over, to keep from getting broadside, overreacting with every stroke so I had to work twice as hard. Broadside would spill me. The beach was behind me. My only choice was to paddle out through the waves or turn and surf the short distance in to shore. But I wanted a long, steady ride, not a dozen shorter ones where I wouldn't even have a chance to catch my rhythm before it was over. So I headed out, and slowly the motion as it was meant to be came back to me. A slight roll at the hip that sent the paddle blade forward through the air, and the roll of the opposite hip to bring the paddle in and back through the water. The wrists alternately cocked; the arms like horizontal pistons, bent, extended, bent, extended. They were the real workers, those arms. My legs lay motionless under the deck of the boat, my knees locked against the sides of the kayak

155

to stabilize it. In the next few hours my arms would be the only part of my body I could look at to see that I was really alive.

A first rush of adrenaline had left its bitter taste on my tongue, and I opened my mouth to the snow and the spray off my paddle. I'd been gone only half an hour and already my wrists and upper arms felt on fire with the work. But if I rested a stroke I veered broadside, and the kayak lost its connection, by the paddle, to the water. Out here the troughs were huge, and getting deeper. There was so much water in the boat I was pulling three times my weight, or more. It stabilized me, but made it hard to maneuver. Hard to flick in a light, correcting stroke and impossible, I knew, to keep the boat upright if it started its slow roll over.

So I laid the paddle across the deck and held onto it with one hand while the other hand bailed. Stupid. I hadn't thought to bring a cup or scoop, and the little I splashed out splashed right back in on the next wave. I would have to use both hands, hook an elbow over the paddle and ride the broadside, adjusting with my hips. I had time to look up as I worked, and time to think. I saw how the circular snow was oddly like a sunrise, the way it hurried up out of blackness to imbue the world with light. I thought of the word *grace,* for some reason. Of the body's grace, often at its most intense when the most is being asked of it, and of that other grace, God's or someone's, that seems to fall on simple people and children. I don't know what that thought might have become. It vanished under the same roller that caught and swamped the boat. I felt the second it happened. It was as if the water threw its head in my lap and pinned me there where I couldn't struggle; I could only say yes to it. But if I'd struggled I'm sure I would have tipped myself over, and this way I was only stunned and waterlogged, with the boat riding just a few inches above the level of the sea—but riding, still upright.

First I noticed that my wool hat was gone. I reached up for it with both hands and this told me I must have lost the paddle too. All right. I will ride this out with my arms, I thought. And keep the ocean in the boat if that's where it wants to be. I can use its weight now as long as I use its movement under me at the same time. Turn yourself. Quiet. Concentrate. Turn the nose to the shore and surf in on the breakers. But the shore is gone, isn't it, Franny? My god. I don't know which direction will take me home.

I had once heard from an old Massachusetts sea captain that the first thing to do if you go overboard is to pee. I did, though I wasn't overboard, and inside the wetsuit I felt a few seconds of what seemed like sunlight on my legs. But the cold, when it came, came on me hard. My upper body felt like an icy skin had been drawn across it and tightened down to where it would have to crack, or suffocate me. I was afraid, for the first time that night. I gasped for air, though there was no lack of it. With the sudden drenching, and without my hat, my sweat had solidified under the wetsuit. I remembered and regretted the long underwear that gripped me now tighter than any person ever had. Even at my core, the only warmth I was aware of was a salty burning in my lungs from having swallowed so much water. But that was enough. That was the candle I had to keep lit. The snow blew horizontal, and over the water now it had turned to a sleety rain.

Go somewhere, I told myself. Try one direction and if that's not right, try another. But the sea was more complicated now than before with its simple in, out and broadside. I felt like the eye of something with waves coming at me from all sides; the uncalm eye of a watery storm. The peaks and valleys of the big rollers had flattened to a sharp, mean chop that made it almost impossible to paddle with my arms. My hands grabbed air as often as water, and two or three times I lost my precarious balance and almost went over.

I heard Esther's "Roll with it, move as it moves," and it clicked in me that the only way to survive the next hours or minutes would be to become the ocean, to embrace it and love it and everything it gave me. So I stopped struggling. My mind stopped struggling. My hands were dull and numb, like two blunt fish as I pulled them out of the sea and rested them on the deck of the kayak. I found I could balance the boat more easily now. Everything, it seemed, had suddenly slowed down.

I still couldn't see anything beyond the nose of the kayak. Black sea and sky and the white connecting rain streamed from one end of the boat to the other, then were gone off into more blackness. I pulled all my concentration to the center of my being, which wasn't the center of my body but a wide stripe across my chest, and with everything in me as still and calmly quiet as I could make it, I listened. I listened for two things. On the outside, I listened for the boom of breakers falling on beach or cliff. I didn't know how I would know the difference in intonation, if there was one at all, though I guessed the sound of water on sand would be higher and softer than water against a face of rock. And on the inside, I listened to the blood and organs of my body, or my imagination of them. I needed to hear the heart pumping, the lungs heaving—even the liver and spleen and god knows what, all working to keep me alive, to warm me. I needed to know my veins and arteries were not frozen shut. I couldn't move around in the boat so the only way to flush my core warmth outward through my body was to will it. What color will it be? I wondered. I set a gold light in motion from my heart, trying hard to remember where it would go next. Old biology textbooks with the route of the blood on one transparency, skeleton and muscles on another, came to me. I set my mind to those pages, absurdly far from where I now drifted, a winter night on the Pacific, and they told me: Out to the lungs! Out to the arms and hands! Out through the torso's winding maze of organs—gold light! To the thighs, knees, shins! To the calves and feet! Feel each toe, Franny. Feel it burning, waking. And the water which is moving around your body in the boat is warmer now, isn't it? Green and gold, and the deep cold gone out of it. A baby in a bathtub, you are, dreaming back into yourself all the dreams it's taken your whole life to pour out. Quiet, rocking body, becoming its boat, becoming its ocean; drifting if not out, then in; if not in, then at least to sleep. Where will it carry you, this storm? How many hours until light? Will the rain die first, or the darkness? As soon as you can see where you're going, use your last little strength to get there. But now, nothing. All a black nothing. Rest. Sleep. Dream of not dreaming. What you are going down under is a tiredness so large you can float up through it again when you hit bottom. Or live in it like a fish. Thick, white blanket, not water, not air, not the blown snow, riding up behind your eyes—it lives where you live, it *is* you, pressing the eyelids shut, weighing down the back of the skull so the throat is a slim white triangle falling up from the wet suit collar.

Franny! I called to myself and jerked upright, forgetting for a second where I was and who belonged to the name I was calling. Right away I recognized where I'd been. I'd called from the bottom of a pit, it seemed, where I'd been carried by my own exhaustion and by the cold. The cold, that thick white blanket that must be the last dream of anyone who has frozen to death. The sea and drowning I wasn't afraid of. I knew I could ride out almost anything I was given if I just held onto the boat. Or lay on the upturned boat if it went over. But the cold could kill me, I was certain. It had already taken me halfway there: It had put me to sleep.

Suddenly I had the fear-sickening feeling of being punched in the stomach, short little blows that kept coming and coming and I didn't try to stop them. I was shivering violently, inside and out. This was the only reminder I had that my body was there, hurting, alive. My ears listened. How long was it? My eyes tried to see through the darkness, but were pushed back each time to the middle of it, into it, where nothing was. Then it came. There was no slow start to it as I had expected. It came in a hollow, singing rush, though no song had ever sounded like that before. No human throat—or animal—was capable of such a noise. I knew at once it was what I'd been listening for, closer than I dared imagine. I knew, too, that it was the wrong half of what I'd hoped to hear. These were breakers exploding against something unyielding and vertical. There was no mistaking the intonation.

I had no idea how much time I had, though I guessed less than five minutes. *Five minutes.* Those words meant nothing to me. Even the nerves alive in my stomach meant nothing, nor the cold I couldn't feel. I thought only of where I might be in relation to the beach, and what my best chance was of getting back there. I knew these cliffs. I had walked and run and lived on top of them. I had looked down from them onto the bodies of sheep and old ship timbers, and once seen a door thrown up between the rocks—a closed door until the sea split it in two. From the beach they ran north for miles, for as far as I'd ever been, and beyond that for as far as I could see. The storm had carried me up the coast, I knew, but how far I had no idea. If the beach were less than half a mile—less than a quarter of a mile behind me, there was a chance, a small one, but a chance that I could turn myself around and paddle like hell with my arms to get back to it. The worst that might happen would be no worse than what was coming up quickly, inevitably on my right; the steady, howling boom of big waves crushing everything in them and with them against the cliffs.

The ocean had turned into its old, deep-troughed self again, closer and closer to the shore. I dug into it up to my armpits, concentrating on my direction above everything else. I could borrow time for myself by heading, or trying to head out to sea while angling south at the same time. I gave myself to it. What could I do but give myself to it? The part of me that thought and overthought, and worried and went inward in tiny, tightening circles, wasn't with me now in the boat as it hadn't been with me in any of the exacting or enlarging moments of my life. I was a free creature, body and mind stroking together through the looming waters, swinging each arm into the center of each oncoming wave like a punch the water would fall under; bending almost flat across the deck of the kayak, the effort pushing me down so I became the boat. I was drenched and only knew it by the water I dragged into my lungs on every breath, so I was gasping, not breathing; and then sobbing with the whole beautiful uselessness of what I was trying to do. I was too small for my plans. I was one tiny creature and here, against me, was the sea.

I fought for I don't know how long. Time had no place there. Time, if it were anything, was the frozen rain turning again to snow. I took this as a kind of sign, the visibility narrowing down to only a small circle around my head—a halo, I thought, and said the word out loud, and laughed with all the strength gone out of me into the bulge of the next high swell. I will not see the wall coming at me, I told myself. At least that. But I couldn't shut down the sound which was more accurate, more ominous than any eyesight could ever have been. I gave up. I folded, I believe I folded, my arms across my chest in a posture of endless patience. But I didn't have to wait long. The waves' momentum caught me and kept me. I surfed several yards, my arms working desperately again to keep me upright. And all about me was sound, noise, the chug, it seemed, of a powerful engine that I was inside of. A wailing, steaming, crunching machine. The crunch was ahead of me still, though I could feel myself inexorably pulled to it. Then the nose lifted. I saw the boat bend back over my head, a black arrow shot up into blackness. I heard a crack like trees breaking, a forest of trees coming down on me, though there was no longer a me, but limbs and neck and head all equal to the exploding rock and water of which my body was a part.

I woke in the sand with my arms wrapped around the front half of the kayak, which was all that was left of it. The sky was a light gray and the sea, thirty yards beyond my legs, still rose and cracked with a terrible, deafening roar. I tried to sit up, tried to claim my body, but it was as if I'd left it somewhere else. The snow had stopped. I saw that I was on a tiny beach, just a scrap of sand interrupting the endless boulders that lined the foot of the cliff. I raised my head and a bolt of pain ran between my shoulders, giving them back to me. To my left, about a mile away, I saw where the cliffs fell down forever onto the sand beach I'd started out from the night before.

Was it the night before? I could tell from the sun that moved weakly behind the gray cloud wall, moved in another world, a world I wanted to be in, not this one, that it was close to the middle of whatever day it was. The air on my face and feet felt cold. It brought those parts back to me. My arms were so locked around the kayak, and my hands so knotted together, I couldn't isolate muscle from bone, nor bone from fiberglass. It took several minutes before I was able to send enough strength to one thumb, and move it. But when it moved, slightly upward and to the right, I remember, every other movement seemed suddenly possible, and the fingers unclasped quickly, stiffly, then the arms let go. The boat slid a few inches down the sand, like a dying fish exhaling its last.

After some time I sat up. A dull, thudding pain was in every part of me, except in my right arm where I felt nothing. I looked at it, as if the arm had nothing to do with me. Even under the wet suit I could see something was terribly wrong about the angle. It ran perfectly from shoulder to elbow, but the elbow had slipped around to the front so the forearm, when I raised it, pointed backwards.

I threw up everything in me, which was only the sea. I wonder what it will feel like when it begins to feel, I said to myself. It better damn well not be before I'm out of here.

I could walk, holding the arm against me, still pointing wrongly and rudely backwards—at the broken shell of the kayak, at the miracle of beach that had come out of god knows where to soften my landing and save my life. While I groped barefoot over and around the seaweed-wet rocks, aware of the speed of the tide's rising and the narrowing path between ocean and cliff, all this time the arm reached behind as if to drag the whole misadventure with me. It played the part of nostalgia, which is never done with the past. I had the sickening feeling, whenever I looked down at it, that it would break off in my hand—or had already inside the wet suit. What would I do then? Take it with me or leave it behind? Heave it, I decided, and all its inarticulate pain, into the sea.

I think I was only half conscious when I reached the beach. The first thing I saw was the kayak's lost spray-skirt caught in some dune grass a few feet from where the boat had been. I knelt down, or the beach came up. I buried my cheek in the damp sand and wanted, suddenly, to bury my whole head but didn't have the strength for it. I lay with a view of a shell, one of those inwardly traveling spirals like a conch or nautilus. It was pink and cream-colored and it filled my world until Esther found me, moments or hours later.

10

I had left the lamps burning and a fine black soot had settled on the windowsill and on the scattered pages of Claire's letter. "That's how I knew to come look for you," said Esther. "The cabin stank of kerosene and there was that letter from your girlfriend on the table."

She was driving me home from the hospital. It was midnight and the roads were snow packed and icy. My arm ached terribly in its new white cast, although the doctors had shot me full of codeine and who knows what else and sent me away with what looked like a year's supply as well. But the pain, which had held off miraculously until Esther had found me and I was halfway back to the cabin in her arms, kept coming. It seemed to know how to make up for itself and I dreaded this night's lying down to sleep.

"Are you exhausted?" she asked me.

I shook my head. "Just drugged." I realized I didn't

know what day it was, whether I'd been out one day or two—or a week. Those details had never been.

"What's the day?" I asked.

"Friday. Well, it's after midnight now. Saturday. The 28th."

"Oh god."

She took her right hand from the wheel and held my good hand with it. "You were out there, wherever you were, about sixteen hours. The pretty-looking doctor told me that. I guess they can tell those things. He said the arm was the least of your problems and that the cold would have killed anyone else." She laughed. "You know, Franny, he had a little crush on you by the time he was all through putting you back together."

I celebrated my birthday by sitting up all night watching Esther sleep. It's sleep that makes us whole, I thought; sleep that turns us into everyone else.

For the next week I was coddled by my friend. The pain in my arm ebbed, my cuts and bruises healed, and Esther and I took walks in a weather that had turned suddenly balmy, a false spring. We avoided the cliffs, though the sound of the sea seemed to infiltrate everywhere. It was days before I could even talk about what I'd done. Esther wasn't at all interested in what had become of her kayak, or in any of the details that made high adventure out of what was, at heart, sheer folly. What she wanted to know was, *Why, Franny? Why, why, why?* And this was the hardest story to tell her because I didn't know myself.

"I don't get it," she said. "Or maybe I get it too well. You get a long letter from your girlfriend and go out and try to kill yourself. Why? You're not a crazy lady. That's what I like about you. It's pitch black and snowing outside and you figure it's perfect weather to go for a boat ride. What kind of nonsense is that?"

"It wasn't nonsense, Esther. It wasn't craziness. It was a mistake."

"You were drunk then. Tell me, were you drunk?"

"Hell no, I wasn't drunk! I was tired, I was sad. I needed to break loose, break out of here! I just didn't think about the weather. I wanted to go lose myself and that was one way to do it. Forget myself. In fact," and this only came to me as I was talking, "that was something I used to do every summer when I was a kid. I'd go throw myself in the waves."

"In the summer," said Esther, "in the daylight, with probably half a dozen cute lifeguards ready to jump, run and save you!"

"No. Just my mother."

"Well, the point is, why do you all of a sudden have to forget yourself when all this time I've known you you've been remembering yourself just fine. Until that wacko—excuse me, but I've got to think there's something not quite right with that woman—sends you what looks like the longest love letter ever written, and you go plunge yourself in the sea!"

"Esther!"

"Well, am I wrong?"

"First of all, it's not a love letter, and second, she's a thing of the past. We're through. We love each other. We're possibly soulmates. And we're through."

Esther, who had never for a minute claimed possession of me, who for months now had been the closest, dearest friend I had, gave up on me. She threw her hands up in front of her and shook her head. "Don't you believe it, Franny. You'd be a fool to believe it. You've got miles to go with that woman."

This was the last said on the subject, and really the last serious exchange between us. True spring arrived. My arm, hidden away where I couldn't see it, slowly knit together again and each time I went to see the doctor I was rewarded with a shorter, less cumbersome cast. I couldn't properly swim, but I could flop in the ocean, and my friend and I went often to the beach, chucked our clothes and stayed the afternoon. Esther went once without me to the little beach where I'd landed, and came back as sober as I'd ever seen her. "You better believe in luck," was all she said. She would count Tule elk again that summer, and I would move on. I was flooded with a spring restlessness and decided I would rather be one-armed in a town or small city than here in the woods.

I went to Santa Fe. Esther, waving both arms madly, shouting well-wishes, disappeared in the rearview, as had Gus and Katheryn, as would some others I'd come to love. Here I was, pushing myself out again, and it only looked like the mirror had gobbled another fondness.

I was a few days on the road, stopping often to water the poor old overheating Futura. In Santa Fe I found a tumbledown house to rent for thirty-five dollars a month in a neighborhood of pink churches and vacant lots. Nobody wanted to hire me at first, then everyone did. I started working for a dance magazine, writing articles, learning how to peck away one-handed at a typewriter. But my tool of preference became the camera. I knew nothing about photography, and no one I worked with had the time or interest to teach me, so I taught myself. It was a balancing act at first. My right arm was worthless, and my left was so unsteady I ruined countless rolls of film. But my awkwardness attracted people, or at least put them at ease in front of the camera. For a long time my best company was what I saw through the lens, and when I turned my bathroom into a darkroom, that same company came up in the developer. It was a miracle to me, and still is, that image afloat in the first tray. I could cure almost any loneliness by printing pictures.

The cast came off. The summer went by, and the autumn. I had occasional short notes from Esther, always hilarious, and weekly typed letters from Katheryn or Gus. Claire told me nothing, though she might have tried. I was fairly certain her communications would get as far as California and no farther as long as Esther was watching out for me.

In Santa Fe I had friends, men and women, who interested me, and lovers who mostly did not, though it was a good town for love. It was a glory and feast for the eyes with its washed adobe and crooked streets dead-ending, as often as not, at a blue door upon which the yellow sunlight bristled. Or opening onto a vacant lot of mullen. My house was surrounded by the stuff, as well as goldenrod and purple horsemint all fall, growing up between the seats of four junk cars belonging to my landlady's husband's cousin's son. In that neighborhood the church bells rang for every occasion: rang the hour, rang fretfully for funerals and shouted out weddings. I loved the brides who stepped across my weeds on their way to be married, and on their way back waved from car windows blaring rock and roll.

Through the winter and into the spring, I loved my life, knowing no one really well and believing the city beautiful beyond my ring of junk cars. I loved the possibility of love, though I didn't seek it out. Instead, I waited. I worked. I walked with my camera and without, learning the well-lit streets by heart and pushing aside stories of racial hate and violence that kept others inside at night. One evening a couple of noisy tanagers led me to the dry ditch behind my house, and I followed it. These ditches, once full of irrigation water, had been to the old Santa Fe what streets and traffic now were to the new—the neighborhoods' vital connections. Mine carried me through willows, box elder, more tanagers and orioles. It carried me into the Acequia Madre, the Mother Ditch, and from there past the back doors of ritzy shops and galleries on Canyon Road. Under a pedestrian bridge, through a park, behind the Spanish movie theater to a side of town I'd never seen before, passed through a hundred times in daylight and never seen. The houses were worn thin with tin sheets thrown up around the adobe to keep the weather out. The dogs were thin and disinterested. And where were the people? Who were they? I wanted to know.

After that I no longer worked at being enchanted. I was less interested in the romance and surface of things. This meant wandering into frightening new places, intruding with my camera and often counting on luck and intuition to get me home. I was a woman. That worked against me. I was Anglo-Saxon, and at twenty-five I still looked ten years younger than my age. People—men— laid their hands on me. Several times I was followed to the edge of the barrio. I had learned enough Spanish to understand how often I was teased or insulted by strangers, but if I'd hated them for it I couldn't have kept going back to photograph.

These were no longer the routine pictures of little girls in tutus scrubbed clean for the lady from the magazine. These were mine, and in them I worked only for myself. There was a natural dance that people did, in anger, in fear, in sorrow, in chasing a dog or child through an alley, and that was what I wanted to record—emotion! Kids came out at me with sticks sometimes, and at other times came with a curiosity that was easy and beautiful to photograph. Day pictures were safer than night, though I always believed the night to be a more genuine medium. I didn't make friends. I was never really trusted. I made many enemies, each of whom taught me more than my acquaintances, friends and lovers in the world beyond the barrio. If I could get a little Spanish kid to stand still for my camera under a Nehi sign while his friends hooted and darted around on their bikes, that was a patience I'd learned.

I became a shadowy figure at the magazine, showing up only to get my assignments in on time: tutued girls, or their mothers puffing and sweating through aerobics. I knew these pictures were heartless, dull and duty-bound creatures. They were also exactly what was expected of me. It is a sad truth about magazine work that anything of spirit is edited out as irrelevant, and this was how I came to see my life beyond the barrio. So I worked harder on my own photographs, which nobody saw—there was no one I trusted to see them—and did enough to get by at work. It was a terrible, hot summer of one dance company after another; the impossible telescopic shot of leg or face taken from a crouch in the aisles. Even then, the best were never printed, the ones showing the real strain and tension behind a dancer's grace. "Aesthetically inappropriate" was what my editors always called the truth. I was happiest when I was being ignored or chased off by some uneasy grandmother whose face in my lens was as tense and grace-ful as any dancer's.

There was another face in my lens, finally, that moved me enough to pursue it. She showed up in a ballet class I was sent off to photograph. I usually dreaded those as-signments that took me into the kingdoms of tiny-waisted women, women who wept in front of mirrors at the gain of a pound. They were all supreme athletes, with terrific stamina and a discipline in their art that boggled me. But what they called "being married to the dance," actually meant being a slave to it. They seemed so joyless to me, and that was difficult and painful to record.

Against this backdrop of Margot Fonteyns, BT stood out like Marco Polo in China. She was a tan, squarish woman with dark hair and a bowl haircut, a frank, easy face. Every-one else was in leotards and leg warmers; she was wearing sweatpants. And no shirt. Just her bra. A lacy black bra that the rest of the class had apparently grown accustomed to. At least it didn't seem to cause a stir in anybody besides me. She had wide hips and shoulders, and arms that looked strong—from milking cows or tossing haybales, that was my immediate thought. I don't know why, in a bra like that, I imagined her on a farm. No one else came close to her, that was all I knew.

She couldn't dance, though she certainly was an athlete, and yet I shot three rolls of her alone and only a couple of uninspired ones of the rest of the class. From the beginning I was shy of her. That was how I knew she moved me. I skirted around the edge of all those first, second, third positions and pliés, catching her in my telephoto and assuming, from her fierce concentration on the back or wall ahead of her, that she knew nothing about it.

But I was wrong. I spent several hours in the darkroom that afternoon and evening, watching her come alive in the developer. I raced through negative after negative, falling in love with that face a little more each time it appeared. I laughed to think that here I was, making it appear! I felt strong and greedy. The next day I waited for her before class. She arrived in the same sweatpants and a sweatshirt covering the black bra. I had some pictures for her, I said. "Yeah, about three rolls," she said. I blushed. I wondered how I could get them to her. "Well, you could have brought them here today, with you," she said. It wasn't working out at all like I imagined. But when she saw that I might give up she wrote her initials and address on a small piece of paper and gave it to me.

"Don't lose it," she told me, and squeezed my hand. "Or memorize it, that way you'll have it forever." She was about to go in. "But I won't live there forever. So come see me soon."

But I was busy the next day, and the next, and a week went by before I had a free evening. I'd blown up the best shots of her, and I carried these and a bottle of wine with me across town to her door at 615 Calle Maria Magdalena. Damn these Catholics, I thought, turning every street or alley into a holy affair with their names. Relentless! I feel watched! BT later reminded me that Mary Magdalene was the prostitute, but at the time I had no such comfort.

It was mid-September, a sweet, clear late afternoon, full of dogs barking, and away up in the Sangre de Cristo Mountains the first touches of snow. It came early in the high places, or never left. Alone up there in the spring, I'd built an igloo and slept in it.

I walked slowly, aware of my nerves, and more and more slowly the closer I came to BT's house. She wasn't expecting me. She might not even be home. She had given me no phone number so I couldn't call her. I stopped for things in the street, things to bring to her. Half a fortune cookie; a tiny doll's head; a pipe cleaner horse. Her neighbor on the right was an old man flattening his hedge with a pair of electric shears. On the left a pajamaed boy and his mother faced each other, fighting over bedtime.

God knows why I didn't knock, why I didn't even approach the door but went around the side of the house instead. Possibly because the door wasn't easy to find that day: BT had washed her shirts and they fluttered from a makeshift laundry line across the front porch. I remember two pink blouses in the middle that surprised me almost as much as the black bra had. I would have had to walk between them to get to that door.

But instead I found a window and looked through it. There was BT, stretched naked on her bed, one hand holding a teacup and the other stroking her crotch. I was so close to her. The window was directly above where she lay. She was already flushed in the face and across her breasts, and she had four fingers up inside her. I liked that. I was impressed by that. Four fingers! I thought, and I thought of the times I'd loved so hard I wanted to bury my head inside a woman, or my whole hand at least.

She stroked slowly. She half raised her beautiful thick hips from the bed, and her stomach muscles tightened and loosened and tightened again, taken by that familiar wave.

She pulled her fingers out and dipped them into the teacup and slipped them back inside her again. She did this several times, and her body and face blushed beautifully, more and more every time she touched herself. Her eyes closed. She looked like an angel to me. Her hand left the teacup and came to join the other, pressed the other hard inside her. I wanted to run in to her. The wave was over her and her mouth said, *Oh, oh,* dying out in little ripples as her body jerked, suddenly too sensitive. Then she was smiling with her eyes closed and the teacup had fallen to the floor.

He was still trimming his hedge when I walked through her front yard and into the street. I realized only a few minutes had gone by. I had thought much longer, but here it was, the color of the sky hadn't changed and an old man had moved only a few steps sideways, following his shears. I laughed out loud, facing number 615 from down the block with no chance of being seen. I wasn't ready for BT yet, and I was certain she wasn't ready for me. I'd give her half an hour.

When I came back the shirts were gone. I knocked this time and she opened the door. She was wearing one of the pink blouses with nothing underneath it, and noticing this, I felt more like a voyeur than when I'd stood at the window watching her.

"Oh my god, it's you," she said. I felt so awkward and out of place and excited, standing in her doorway. I shoved the photographs at her, and the bottle of wine, then one at a time the little presents I'd picked up off the street. But they'd changed. They no longer looked like gold to me, just gutter junk. I turned the color of her blouse.

"You blush a lot." She squatted down and put the photographs on the floor, the other things next to the photographs, very carefully, not in any way rushed; as slowly, I thought, as I'd seen her stroking herself. And when she stood up she had both arms free for me and wrapped me in a most welcome, most magnificent hug.

She was a few inches taller than me, at least a few years older, and in her house that evening a lot more relaxed. "Are you on your way out somewhere?" I wanted to know.

"Yeah. You can stay, though."

"Well, I . . ."

"No, I mean you can stay and I'll stay with you!"

I wanted to know what her real name was, and we realized she didn't know mine. "Franny," I told her. I laughed. "F."

"Barbara Theresa," she said. "Actually, Barbara *Louise* Theresa."

"Another Catholic?" She nodded. "And why do you call yourself BT?"

"I couldn't live with Barbara, Louise or Theresa, and BLT was out. That left BT. And here I am."

As far as I remember we never stopped touching each other after that first hug. She led me by the hand around her tiny house, to the kitchen, to the bathroom, to the bedroom I'd already seen. It was much more comfortable than what I was used to, with satiny pillows in every room and decent lamps and a deep black bathtub that reminded me of BT's bra. The bedroom was painted fuchsia, what she called "cunt pink." There was a mirror over the dresser and a long mirror where I imagined her naked, bobbing up and down in those jerky pliés I'd first loved her for. The bed was unmade. On a small table next to it there were oils and incense, some bracelets and a bowl of feathers.

"You haven't eaten," said BT. It wasn't a question. "I'll make you something called The Enchanted Broccoli Forest. You're not afraid of broccoli, are you?"

She was an excellent cook. I should have known that, but those dirty sweatpants of our first encounter had left their impression, and kept coming up to throw me off. We drank my wine, then half a bottle of hers. She did most

of the drinking, I did most of the talking. She excited me.
I told her about the barrio, my art—things I hadn't told
anyone. I said nothing about love. We held hands all through
that meal. Under her table I rested my bare feet on hers.
Finally she talked about her present lover, Marion.

"Would she mind this?" I asked, feeling stupid, tightening my grip on her and feeling at the same time the
electric charge that had never stopped running between
our bodies.

"If she did I wouldn't be doing it." BT shook her
head. "We're not monogamous. Even when we lived together we were allowed to have affairs."

"Is it easy for you?"

"Is what easy for me?"

"To touch people. To have affairs. To go to bed with
people?"

"If I love them, honey, that's always been easy. But
there just aren't a whole lot of people I love. I mean my
soul pouring out." She tapped her breastbone. "I mean
this."

"Isn't it funny. We don't even know each other."

After supper BT closed all the curtains in the house
and set up her massage table. She wanted to give me something for the photographs. She took her shirt off. I undressed down to my underpants. "Underpants off," she
said. She laughed. "You have a beautiful butt, Franny.
Hasn't anyone ever told you that?"

And in the hour I was touched by her, I had beautiful
shins, beautiful hipbones, elbows, clavicle, cheeks. Wherever she massaged me, and felt me give in to her, she felt,
and I felt, too, the beauty and power of my body. I shone.
I really believe that night I gave off light. And when she
finished she pulled the sheet up over me and stood by my
head, holding both my hands. "You are dazzling." She
leaned over and kissed my lips. Her breasts brushed my
shoulders. "You are so willing," she told me. "You should

touch yourself every day, sweet woman. You should take care of yourself with your hands. You deserve that."

I had my eyes closed. I felt in the presence of some beautiful nurse or angel. I suddenly remembered her that afternoon, and I ached for her.

"What was in the teacup?" I asked. She didn't answer. "That you dipped your fingers in when you were masturbating?"

"Franny!"

I opened my eyes. "I saw."

"You *saw!*" She was blushing, as pink as I'd seen her that afternoon.

"You blush a lot," I said. I was laughing. So was she. I reached for her ears and pulled her face down to mine.

"Why you little spy," she whispered. "You little peeping tom."

We were so hungry for each other it was almost comical, and because BT couldn't or wouldn't, I found in myself some surprising power to go slow. She carried me off to her bed. I felt the solidity of her arms, of her whole body, easily lifting me and setting me down in her sheets. I was naked already. She was half. It seemed an hour I kissed those beautiful breasts of hers, their perfect roundness swelling under my tongue. She was ticklish everywhere. She had a wonderful, musty cunt which opened and opened for me, for my tongue, for my fingers. "Love me," she whispered, and I loved her harder and harder until she rippled and rose and sank, her head turning from side to side on the pillow. She lifted her face. "Come to me, come to me," and pulled me up so I lay with my breasts on hers, our bellies together. She lifted her knee and pressed it into my crotch. "You're so good," she said. "You're a dream."

We slept holding each other. I was a little lost in the morning, the way I always was with a new lover. I told BT this and she said, "It's social conditioning, that's all."

176

"That doesn't help me much," I said.

"What would help?"

"If we made love again."

And as soon as we were in each other's arms, it was all right. I wasn't afraid of her, of our differences, of her fuchsia bedroom and floor-length mirror; or her life with Marion; or how long I'd have her, my comfort, the sweet sex. Here she was. Nothing else mattered. We were strangers, and yet our bodies might have known and loved each other for years.

A few hours later, after she'd brought me breakfast in bed and we sat drinking her good, strong coffee, feeding each other the last English muffin, she told me about herself. I said, "Tell me your best kept secret, BT."

She thought a moment. "I'm not sure anything's a secret anymore. I was married for eight years. I have two kids, beautiful kids, a boy and a girl. They live with their father, who is a decent man, just not worth being married to."

"Two kids!"

"Yep."

"Good god. Do you ever see them?"

"A couple of times a month. They live in Los Alamos now. Their father drops them off. I spoil them. We have a good time together, and then they go home."

"Sad."

"Not really. They're doing fine. I'm doing fine. Michael's doing fine. He wanted them, I didn't. We both knew he could support them better than I could, at the time. I wasn't working. I didn't have a skill. It's just in the last couple of years, since the divorce, that I've learned anything at all about getting and keeping money. It's hard to learn that in a marriage. It's hard to learn a lot of things."

"So you can earn a living with the massage?"

"Massage? Hell no, honey, I'm an electrician! I'm Union. I earn nine-eighteen an hour rewiring hospitals and motels. Or working for rich people."

I was laughing. "I don't believe it."

"Sure! I've got a tool belt. Want to see my tool belt?"

And she did. This marvelous, sensuous, sexy woman had a tool belt. She brought it out of the closet and showed it to me. She was an electrician. I never dreamed she'd be an electrician. A natural healer, a masseuse—I was sure of it. I shook my head at her. "All I can say is you've got a lot of wattage in your hands."

But she was serious. "See, that's all social conditioning, Franny. Even you, wide-minded you, can't believe you've just gone to bed with an electrician; have just wolfed down a breakfast—eggs cooked to perfection, muffin not burned— brought lovingly to your bed by an electrician. That's crazy! Don't you see how crazy that is? I mean not you, the world we live in; the patriarchal world we live in. Tell me it's not crazy!"

"Wait, BT, please," I said. "You're losing me. You have no idea how nervous I get around politics. I'm scared of angry feminists and big political dykes." My god, Franny, I thought to myself, how long have you known that's true and never said it, even to yourself?

But BT had already lightened up. In fact her anger was this way, here and gone, and I admired her for it. Politically, she wasn't any less serious than anyone else, but she had a sense of humor, something so many of her friends, whom I would meet, tragically lacked.

"Well," she said, "you aren't afraid of the word 'dyke' at least. How long have you loved women?"

"Three years. Three good years."

"Want to say anything else about it?"

I shook my head. "Not at the moment."

"Well whenever you do, I'll listen. Honey, I'll be here to listen."

I loved that woman, openly, inwardly, through all the flesh and bones of her and out through her strong, electrician's hands. When I wasn't with her, the hands were what I thought of, rubbing me, warm on my body; and those same hands cutting wires or wrapping black tape, rigging current enough to light up a heart ward—or a bedroom; somebody's lovemaking. Her story, she said, wasn't so incredible. There were women everywhere out there whose story it was too. She'd been a lesbian for years— forever. She married to convince herself otherwise, and when that didn't work, when she found herself still falling in love with women and sneaking around to be with them, she thought children might cure her. She was living in Alaska at the time. Her husband and all her lovers worked in a cannery. She was tired of him, tired of the husky, aggressive women who were her only relief from him. Except in her kids, there just wasn't much place anymore to exercise her heart.

She had friends in Oregon, lesbians who gave her shelter after she left her husband. She brought the girl with her, left the boy. Everyone was unhappy for the next year and a half. Then the Oregon household moved to Santa Fe and she moved with them, began to heal herself, heal her family. She sent the girl back to join her brother and father who were living in Montana. After the divorce they all got closer, emotionally, geographically. "Michael's still a prick," said BT, sitting up next to me in the bed, tickling my face with a feather. "But he's a good father. And the woman he imported after I left him isn't a wicked stepmother. Unenlightened—oh god!—but she loves the hell out of the kids. That's all I care about."

"When did you know you weren't like everyone else?" I asked her.

"Oh honey, I don't think I ever didn't know! But there was something," she grinned. "A beautiful little book called *The Secret Summer* by a woman named Virginia Jaynes. When I read that I realized she was writing about me, which meant there was an us out there, and that's quite a comfort to a twelve-year-old kid. Here," she threw the covers off us both. "I still have it." She was gone in the other room for a minute and came back with a thin, well-used book in her hands. Someone had written out and pasted the word *Dictionary* on the front cover.

"Yeah, I was a little paranoid," she said, lost who knows where for a moment in a memory triggered by her own twelve-year-old scrawl.

"But, BT, it's the wrong shape for a dictionary anyway."

We both laughed. "I was a kid, honey. I wasn't worried about the details. I carried this damn book everywhere for a few months, that's all I remember—reading it, rereading parts of it until I had it memorized. And then I didn't care who caught me with it because they'd never see what I saw in it anyway, and even if they took it away from me I still had it." She tapped her head. "Implanted in my brain."

She didn't recite it, though I believe she could have. She knew exactly what she was looking for, and flipped to it. "Ahem," she cleared her throat, and if either of us had giggled we would have been a couple of schoolgirls tasting their first forbidden prose. "Let me set the scene. Stephen, the boorish young man, has just ravished Julia in the graveyard. It's a warm summer night, a good night for a picnic. They've just finished fucking on the grass. Are you with me, Franny?"

"Absolutely."

"Okay. Here we go. The only other thing I need to tell you is that at the time I read this I had a paper route, not in Kentucky, but close enough to imagine, in Ohio. You'll see." She squeezed my arm. "Now you're twelve, remember. The world, big joke, is about to be your apple. It's a Sunday. Once again you've let them drag you off to Mass, but now you're alone at last in your room, stretched luxuriously on the bed with one hand in your crotch while you read:

"Julia had a sense of all the space in the world having opened up for her. The leaves shook above their heads, giving and taking away the view of the first faint stars. She could go on like this forever, she thought, living in the good sex feeling. But as Stephen rolled over on his side to look at her and call her pretty, the thing in her that was most her went under. He was whispering to her, still calling her pretty and beautiful, and all she was feeling was the loss.

"With this man she loses ten years. Ten years are gone from her body and she is fourteen again, delivering papers through the whitewashed streets of a southern Kentucky town. The streets give onto fields, and the fields give onto a richness of woods and river. The sun's heat diminishes at this time of day as she pedals lightly and easily from yard to yard, no longer damp in her skin, but crusty with the salt sweat. Here a dog comes out to greet her or drive her off, there a little girl in a blue pinafore sings, swinging her dolly. The day is gone, but the night is not yet night. She knows limbo. She knows a momentary freedom where nothing is named.

"Madeleine comes out on her porch, sweeping up the dead leaves of the magnolia. She is in her twenties. Julia has made love to her a hundred times in her mind, with every toss of her arm that sends the paper flying to her porch or bushes. Now she raises the paper-flinging hand back behind her head, thinking of the hidden folds of the older girl's crotch, and hurls it. The rubberband breaks mid-flight and news-sheet flies all over the yard. She gets off her bicycle and Madeleine comes down the steps to help her. With the bicycle against her, Julia stands stiff and still and cannot bend nor move in any way with Madeleine's breath that close to her leg. As the older girl leans over the warm ground to gather sports and politics and fashion into her arms, Julia wants her.

" 'Won't you help me?' says Madeleine, but Julia can do nothing nor feel anything until she is pedaling as hard and fast as she can out of town in the direction of the setting sun, feeling the warm air cool her hot forehead and wishing for some simple release. She rides the bicycle right out into the middle of a field of tobacco and falls off it, touching herself madly before she is even on the ground.

"She is drenched by her youth. Night after night she flies out into a field, or off into the dark stand of hickories along the river. Sometimes it's Madeleine she dreams of, but more often it's a girl of her own invention whom she makes love to, as she makes love to herself. She undresses, and moves face-down in the old leaves, or in the loose dirt at the edge of the tobacco. The girl her mind imagines has the perfect parts of every girl or woman she's ever seen. Her mother and sister are in her, and Madeleine, and the black women who pass her on the edge of town as evening arrives, on their way to errands, speaking slowly out of their wide, soft mouths. They call her 'chile' or 'honeychile' with a richness and mystery that flames Julia's imagination. She passes by them in a heat, no matter how cool and quiet the coming evening, and a mile later she falls onto the ground, shivering, spilling over, catching earth in her mouth, earth mixed with her own saliva, and tasting all there is to taste of it while the depth and passion of fourteen pass through and through her."

BT closed the book and closed her eyes. "I used to masturbate to that the way some people masturbate to music."

I let out a long sigh that sounded as if I'd been

punctured. "It's wonderful stuff. It really is. 'Drenched by her youth' and all. All that passionate South. So different than what I was reading at twelve. I'm embarrassed to tell you."

But BT knew. "*The Hardy Boys,*" she said. "Like every other unconscious baby dyke."

I nodded. "Those and *The Odyssey*. Homer for kicks, can you imagine that? Where did you ever find this treasure?"

"My seventh-grade teacher gave it to me. She just handed it to me one day and said, 'Read this. And keep it.' "

"My god! What sort of school did you go to?"

"Parochial school. Run by the nuns. Her name was Sister Mary Helen, God bless her face and brains and body. She was my Madeleine, and she was looking out for me. She was my guardian angel."

And you mine, I thought. Mine of the moment. It was noon before we got up, got dressed, finally finding our clothes in a tangled heap under the massage table. "Look," I pointed at our two shirts on the floor in a night-long embrace.

It was a brilliant Saturday. We walked out into it arm in arm, hand in hand, unwilling to hide what other lovers never needed to in the world of women with men. We walked out into their world. This was new for me, this public affection, and at first I thought BT did it as an act of defiance until I saw how completely natural it was to her. In one narrow street a couple of young boys looked after us as we passed and hissed, "Faggots!" This was also new for me. But BT was purely practical, not the least angry, if anything, amused. "Error in gender," was all she said.

Where were we going that day? It didn't matter. In fact, I remember almost nothing of what we did, what we saw, ate, drank or talked about until the afternoon was just a painter's smudge between two halves of darkness. By then we were in the barrio. I remember suddenly seeing the adobe turn cold. And then the cold came down from above as well, a whole dark sky of it.

"We don't belong here anymore," I told my friend. She didn't answer. She just kept walking and I walked with her, deeper and deeper into a neighborhood that couldn't hold us, where without my camera I felt vulnerable now as I never had before. I was filled with premonition. "At the Nehi sign," I said, "we'll turn around."

There were radios going inside every house—disco, mariachi and Sinatra mixed with the smell of fried beef and the sweet smell of dried red peppers. The yards were fenced. Chained dogs ran behind the fences. We turned down Calle San Miguel, a thin street with thin sidewalks and shopfronts crowded together, lightless, airless. I knew my way here. Left, then left again on Calle Ortega. We saw the Nehi sign ahead of us and stopped under it for a moment, and kept walking. We didn't say a word. BT walked close against me, not holding my hand now but making sure our arms touched.

She led me, as unafraid of this world as she was of the world outside her house. They were equal to her, equally unlike her, and because she knew she could survive in one, this carried her through the other. I had a scare, we both did, when a parrot shrieked from a covered cage a few yards from us. "Jesus!" I whispered. I stopped dead and clutched her shoulder.

She nodded. "What an ungodly noise."

We went home and she wanted to see my photographs. We sat on the floor of my lampless, single-chaired house, going through my boxes. She moved slowly, thoughtfully. She wanted to see everything I'd ever done, every picture I'd ever made. I studied her face, beautiful and clear even in the unfocused overhead light, and I had the sense, as she bent over one photograph's details or oddities, that I was watching her watch me. She had a lot

184

to say about them. "You're trying too hard in this one," or "Sometimes you're just enduring these people for the sake of their pretty faces, aren't you?" And she was never wrong. Where there was laziness or dishonesty on my part, she caught it. When I wasn't being true to what was in front of me, she knew. She also caught the really fine work that most of it was, though at the time I wasn't sure of it. And she praised me for it.

"Let me come with you, Franny, next time you go out to shoot. I want to see you at it. I bet you're beautiful with all that equipment flying around and everything in you centered in the eyes."

I laughed. "I get pretty wild, actually, though the best pictures I make are the ones made in calm. Even the calm of knowing the shoe's being thrown at me, and within the second will hit me and hit the camera unless I turn my shoulder. I haven't told you the story, BT, about the woman in spiked heels who tried to ruin my day."

She shook her head. "No, but if I go with you I'll protect you." She was smiling, but I knew she was serious. "Two women together are an awful lot stronger and safer than one alone. Now give me a kiss. I'm going home."

"After that speech? You can stay if you like, you know."

"I'd like. Oh, Franny, I'd really like. But Saturday nights I spend with Marion. Now when can I see you again? Can I see you again? Honey, what's the long face?"

The long face was jealousy. The long face was hurt pride. BT knew this and did what she could to comfort me, that strong embrace. She didn't whisper anything in my ear, those words "Trust me," which I've never trusted, or "Believe me," which I've never believed. She just held me. She rocked me. She seemed to understand that it was a hard world I'd just moved into, her world.

"BT," I said. She was outside my door, leaning in to kiss me once more on the chin. "You never answered my question."

"Close your eyes." She moved her lips across one eyelid, then the other. "What question?"

"I asked what was in the teacup."

She pulled her head away, laughing. "My god! you never quit, do you? Milk. Milk was in the teacup."

"Milk?" I repeated. "Why milk?"

"It's thicker than spit and it won't get you pregnant, that's why."

Walking backwards, waving, she crossed my yard, crossed each rectangle of window light, crossed the path of one junk car speeding nowhere. At the end she pushed both palms at me like a person signaling ten with their fingers and she yelled, dear BT, as loud and clear as any church bell in that good, Catholic neighborhood: "I love you, Franny! I love your body! Even if I won't sleep with you tonight!"

THREE

II

This was the winter I looked into the eyes of a stranger, some hirsute man in a wool coat waiting for the same bus as I, and saw in the black of his pupil that he and I and everyone else was just an elaborate nothing. I could have reached down through his eyeball and into his lonely self. I could have waved my arm inside the emptiness of him. Our surroundings invented us, and our friends, I saw, in order to walk through the dark with decent company. This man, I could have changed his name. I could have changed his life all around; in fact, everyone he'd ever met had always done this. He didn't know what to believe any more than I did.

I made some choices and I lived more passionately after that, more impulsively within the choices I had made. I moved out of my house and into BT's, and when I didn't love her enough I willed myself to. No one ever loved anyone enough. No one could promise anything to anyone.

Sometimes I lay perfectly still with my head between her thighs, not wanting to make love to her but only to bury myself inside her body, to crawl up into some holy place. "Life is *hard*," I whispered. "Life is hard, Franny," she whispered back. I often hadn't a clue what I was meant for, and I saw that nobody did.

I saw, I saw. I saw that the adult heart was a steadier, perhaps kinder, but duller animal than its kid self, and when it was time to throw it somewhere we threw it. And we willed it to stick, at least I did. I gave it a strong foothold in my lover. I gave it a place in my photography. Gus and Katheryn visited in February and for a few moments that week I gave it like I had never before given it to them. I sat on the bed in the hotel room while my father produced his old tonsorial scissors. He wrapped my neck with one of the hotel towels.

"You like doing this, Dad?"

"Mmm," he said, and grabbed my head with both of his hands and slowly started pulling my hair. He pulled it back from my forehead and up from my neck. My whole scalp tingled. He ran his fingers around my ears and pulled the lobes hard and suddenly, so my face tilted up and there was his, and beyond his the cream white hotel ceiling.

"It's me, Fru," he whispered. "Your old coach. Your old, old father."

He was almost a blind man. The cataracts had grown up in his eyes so the pupil wasn't the eerie black of every other hollow person in my world, but a clear and ghostly gray. Katheryn was in the bathroom getting dressed and I had to talk him through most of the haircut. "You're risking your life," called my mother. "We're doing fine," I called back. More than once I had to put my hand over his on the scissors and push it away from my ear.

I tried hard to discount the past that winter. It seemed only a precarious way of holding and shaping the present. Gus went home and had his heart attack and left me with a ragged haircut that was more of him than any of my memories of him could be. The snow fell ceaselessly on the town, covering everything. It helped me. It grew up out of the yard in deep drifts until finally I forgot where a certain bush or stone or even the neat rock path to BT's house had been.

"When you get yourself down to nothing," I asked BT, "what's left of you?"

"Nothing?" she asked.

"Without history. With no forevers. With just your skin."

She was laughing. "Well, you could always try living, Franny. That's one way to spend your life."

For a long time after that there were oracles on every corner, pointing the way to the world. The bearded man at the bus stop was the first. The others were like him. They all seemed to wear dark coats and often they carried heavy packages. Only one of them uttered anything at all, a woman outside the A&P who struggled to get up off her knees as if she'd been praying. She was an old blonde and her coat had a blond fur collar, and she shrieked, not at me, but at a man and boy going into the store who tried to help raise her and fell themselves on the ice. The man rolled over on his hip, hitting the ice with his fist and cursing. The boy looked embarrassed and got himself up before the man did because he didn't pound the ground and cry.

Ah, poor people, I thought. Poor dumb souls. We're all just waiting to be more than we are, and most of us will die waiting. What we have here, Frances, is one world, this kneebound old woman, this angry man and boy. But at the heart of this world there's another world, I know it.

I knew it because I'd been in it, through my childhood and half my twenties. My life had been taken up by acts of imagination, which was what I sensed the loss of now. As a kid in a winter storm the snow was the tiger I rode

191

around inside of and everything I saw was crossed by the bare white verticals of its ribs: That was the other world. Where my imagination flew out and increased all possibilities. How long it had been—it had been months since I had felt whatever that was, that catfight in my stomach that signaled the moment of the creative act; the warning that something other than ordinary life was available to me. That shining. Sometimes it took the form of an expanded depth perception, as if the eye or camera could see behind objects. Sometimes it rose up in language, so each word meant at least four things. Sex gave it to me only partially, and only some sex, my more celibate sex, never mine with BT. What I'd lost in my living was some kind of blessed state, and though longing had never brought it back to me, I longed for it suddenly with all my heart.

At home that afternoon I lay for a long time on BT's bed—I still thought of it as her bed—looking up at her fuchsia ceiling. Nothing in or outside of me moved. Not a memory. Not a wish. Not even that longing of less than an hour before to live a charmed life again, to inhabit my imagination. I might have dozed. I don't know how long she had been out there knocking, but for a long time after I heard it I thought it was the noise of the lilac scraping the house.

She finally let herself in and called hello from the doorway. I didn't hear the door shut. A rocket of cold air swept into the bedroom. I called out, "Is that you, Marion?" Marion was the only woman I knew who considered the unlocked houses of her past lovers an invitation. But there was no answer. I heard the door close. For only a second I waited for someone to come in and kill me, then I rushed up and into the next room, for some reason still clinging to the blanket that covered me, and pulled open the front door. She had had time to get as far as the street but she'd only gone a few steps. She was a tall woman wearing rubber boots and the kind of yellow rainjacket sailors wear. Her hair was very short and covered by a cotton handkerchief. She had a long neck and there was a lot of neck showing above the collar of the jacket. I thought how cold she must be. She turned around and faced me and even then I didn't see. The snow in the front yard shone viciously behind her. I only knew it when she walked to me, her old walk, the walk of a growing boy. Just those few steps. I held up the blanket and wrapped her neck with it and pulled her to me, inside.

"That snow makes my eyes hurt," she said. Claire said. A very real, trembling, cold-faced being whom I held onto and who held onto me for a long, long time. The door was at her back and we leaned against it. I felt how thin she'd become. "I'm going to hate letting go of you," she said, and held me harder. "After we let go we'll be all awkward and afraid of each other, won't we?"

"Shh . . . I know, I know."

I made her some toast and gave her one of BT's thick sweaters to wear. She smelled the sleeve and said, "This can't be yours, Franny."

"It's not. It's Barbara Theresa's."

"Who's Barbara Theresa?"

"My lover, Claire."

"Oh. I thought her name was Marion."

"Which is why you ran away so quickly just now."

"I didn't run away, dear girl, I walked. I walked very slowly. I came a long way to find you and then in the end I wanted it to be you who found me."

She had come a long way and without stopping, which explained why she was dressed for a tropical storm instead of the coldest winter Santa Fe had seen in years.

"You're home early."

"By more than a year," she said. "But that's another story."

"Will you tell it?"

"Sometime I'll tell it. Sometime soon."

"And how did you find me?"

"Katheryn led me to you."

"Katheryn?" I said. "Katheryn who?"

Claire laughed. "Katheryn your mother. Very odd, isn't it? It turns out her intuition is the best guarded secret she has. I got a letter from her before I left the islands. It was mostly about you, about some photography show you're having. She said I might want to write to you. She included your address. I don't know how in the world she remembered mine, or knew I was still out there."

"She found out from me," I said.

"From you!"

"That was right before Gus died."

"Your father?" I nodded. "That's sad."

"He asked where you were and I told him, and he must have told her. Mother was extending herself at the time. She went all soft. It was amazing to see."

"I knew it, Franny. I had dreams about her where she was you. I loved that woman."

"Oh Claire, that's ridiculous. She was a witch when you met her, she and her terrible dogs. You didn't love her. She drove you crazy. Come on."

"After the thing about the jack-in-the-pulpits I loved her. Gus was the one I didn't get along with." Claire shrugged. "It doesn't much matter now, does it? I'm sorry about your father. I'm happy about your mother. I'm overjoyed to see you. Do you think we can stop talking about other people now?"

I suddenly remembered having an argument with Claire in her apartment in New York, and how in the middle of it she'd rested her forehead on the white door of the refrigerator and said just that: Do you think we can stop talking about other people now? A confusion of past swept through me. It was a physical sensation, a lot like boredom. I felt as if my limbs wanted to stretch, but couldn't. My mouth felt dusty; my head felt useless and huge. I had imagined this scene many times. God knows, in the two and a half years she'd been gone it would have been hard not to. But I'd always imagined my friend arriving in summer or spring, deeply tanned and wearing hibiscus flowers in her hair. She would be singing, waving, the old Claire, carrying a carved coconut in one hand and a ragged carpetbag in the other—my world traveler, with stories to tell of parrots and headhunters and naked kids diving in the lagoon, and crazed monks and witch doctors, and how I'd been missed, terribly, from the moment she'd stepped on the plane. In the beginning, I let myself imagine she would come back to be with me, but after I hurt my arm I willed those thoughts away. And if I thought of her at all this winter it was almost coincidental, those brief, intuitive wanderings triggered by the sound or smell or sight of her in someone else. Which made her nothing but real now, sitting on a kitchen chair with one boot off, leaning over her knees. I wanted us never to speak, to die this way with everything ahead of us, with the taut tendons of her wrists and hands pulling forever at that stubborn second boot. But it gave, and the rubber hit the floor with a dull thwack, and she said, "I've got the farm, Franny, and I'd like you to come be with me." She said it to the floor, to the boot, to the bottom rung of her chair. Her head came up slowly and I must have looked puzzled. "The farm," she repeated.

"I don't know of any farm, Claire."

"Nora's place. It's in my letters."

"I didn't get your letters," I said. "I only got one of your letters."

She nodded slowly. "You didn't get my letters. You don't know about Nora."

"Who is she? A lover, Claire? An island romance?"

My friend blushed. "When she died in December she was eighty-two. She was the matriarch, my mother's oldest cousin, and she lived and worked alone on her little place in Iowa. She had gardens, I remember, and a few mean hogs. There was a lovely old wide barn she used to call Mae West. We were close, off and on, for some reason, and before Christmas she wrote and asked if I'd be willing to take on the farm. I walked out in a typhoon to send her a telegram. Three words: *A welcome albatross.* I don't know whether she died before or after that bird landed in her lap."

"It's pretty, Claire, but it's much too pretty."

"What's pretty?"

"To think I'd come be with you. *Me?* Come be with *you?* I almost killed myself once trying to get to you. Look." I held out both arms in front of her, afraid she wouldn't believe me. "I almost ruined my arm. The right one's shorter by an inch now."

A sound came out of my friend as if she'd been slapped on the back. "Oh, arm," she said. "Poor, sweet arm." She put her hand under my right wrist as if to weigh it. "What happened?"

"It doesn't matter."

"It matters," she said. "But you're not going to tell me, are you?" I shook my head. "All right, Franny, if we ever get old together that story will be the one fresh thing we didn't use up."

"You really think we'll get old together, don't you? We won't get old together, Claire. Look around you. Look where we are."

"In your lover's house."

"Yes! and I live here too!"

"Dear Franny, I know that!"

One thought crossed my mind: She is not about to look away from me this time. And another: Something is gone in her and it may be a good thing.

I had my hands on the kitchen table and my head on my hands. Claire sat next to me, old friend, smoothing my hair. I turned my cheek to the side so she could hear me. "You're not going to win me back," I whispered. "You're

196

too late. I can't come with you, Claire. I'm with someone else now."

Her hand stopped stroking for a moment. "Bring her along. I'd like to love her too. Bring her with you."

"Be serious, Claire."

"I'm quite serious."

"Listen," I said, "you've been gone too long. People like you are extinct now. They went out with the sixties. What is this? Some kind of commune you want to get started up there? Sheep and goats and cottage industries, and women walking naked through the fields of alfalfa?"

"Sounds lovely."

"Where do you get your ideas?"

"Old farm journals," she said. She was laughing. "And God."

"That does it!" I shot up from the table. "You've got religion now. Don't preach to me, Claire, I beg you. Leave me out of this!"

She shrugged. "You're still the best thing I know, Frances, which is why I came to offer you the best spot in the house. Or if you won't take the house, the barn. And if religion is the me of me then yes, I've got religion. So do you, you idiot. So does a duck."

"A platypus," I said.

"What?"

"Religion killed the platypus."

"Fran?" She waved her hand in front of my face. "What are you saying? Are you awake or asleep?"

I just looked at her, my friend. How beautiful she'd become; her eyes wider, her shoulders stronger. Older. She was a few years into her thirties now and she finally looked her age. Parts of her did. Her face did. She'd worn it around in places I'd never seen and couldn't even imagine. Strangers had known her better than I did now. I leaned over her shoulder and put my face against her neck. My hands held her upper arms. "I'm sorry," I told her, "but you don't mean enough to me anymore to argue."

"Well, it's about time."

As I hung over her she sang me a song. It was a strange little song about a pharaoh. It was tuneless, as all Claire's songs were. I often thought she made them up as she went along, songs about fish, songs about shoes and weather and electrical appliances. Her songs seldom involved people, and never ordinary people, unless by the end of the song they acquired some kind of magical powers. Alice, for example, sat in her bathtub, a sweet little girl, and then by the second verse she'd grown thin enough to slip down the drain. According to Claire, she loved it down there in the sewers. She rode around on the backs of goldfish and alligators.

"Alligators!"

"Yes, of course, Franny. City kids bring them home as pets, baby alligators, and their mothers flush them. They live on sewer rats and grow big and strong."

But that was years ago, and now Claire sang me a song about a king and a feather, a king so ordinary that by the second verse he'd died. "And he stood shivering by the river," she sang, "and the boatman charged him a dollar he didn't have. And the boatman asked him if he'd been weighed but this was the kind of king who knew nothing about the afterworld, nothing about the fee for crossing the river, nothing about the scale of judgment. 'Hop up,' said the boatman, and the king climbed into the golden teacup, as large as his royal chariot. It hung from one arm of a giant scale, and from the other hung a teacup exactly the same, and in that teacup in place of a king, rode a feather, a breast feather of a snowy egret. And the king, lucky soul, felt himself lifted. High up above the river he was lifted, above the boatman, above the charcoal pits and snake pits and drowning holes of hell, until the only thing he could see below him was the feather in the teacup.

He was lighter than that. That was his whole sight and seeing it he flew into heaven.

"That's a true story," said my friend.

"It sounds like the Wizard of Oz."

"That was a true story too. Franny?"

I was still draped around her neck, but now I let go and moved in front of her. At another time I would have wanted to sit in her lap. "Here," she used to say. "Come right here," and she would hold me to her like a child on her knee. But now when she said it, "Come right here," I just pulled my chair up close to hers and sat very straight and still in it, like an animal sniffing the wind.

"I feel like for no particular reason the last few minutes have changed our lives," she said. "Do you?"

"Oh no, Claire. The last few years did that for us. These last few minutes were easy."

"Wasn't it easy to move in with your lover and call that home?" I just stared at her. "Wasn't it?"

I shook my head. "Claire, you are guilty of a great forgetting. If I'd had a home three years ago you never would have moved into it. That takes a certain courage you just don't have."

"But you do."

"Now I do."

"You moved in with me once, Franny."

"That was different," I said. "I adored you. I didn't even know you."

"Ah."

"In the beginning, Claire, and I've never confessed this to anyone, what gave me the courage to be with you was the feeling that because we were women it didn't count."

"It didn't count!"

"Yes. That a woman could never lose anything to a woman, and to really be with someone you had to lose everything."

"Oh, my poor little misguided thing! And do you still believe that?"

"The second, yes," I said. I laughed. "The first, definitely not. I lost years to you. For a long time after you were gone I felt like I'd had a heart operation."

"But 'lose,' Franny? What does that mean, 'lose'?"

"Well, at its best it happens to equals. This is the only way it can happen well. I lose myself by giving myself away."

"You mean by revealing yourself?"

I nodded. "It's a donation, from my open self. No strings. Gus taught me that, though I didn't see it until after he died."

"Maybe it took that to make you equals."

"What? His death?"

"Yes," said Claire. "You have a bad habit, Franny, of making the ones you most love bigger than life, and calling that distance their distance rather than yours. What if you'd really gotten close to Gus, as close as he always wanted, and found out he was a fraud. Or just dull. Or a mediocre cook. Where would that have left you? Out looking for another father, right?"

"What are you getting at, Claire?"

"Equality." She said the word as if its syllables were four flat stones. "You worshipped me and you worshipped Gus, and that was all just a way of not being in a relationship with us. You have more of a thing going with Katheryn, believe it or not, than with either of us. You're not afraid to see her flaws."

"Oh bullshit!"

"It's true, Franny."

"Why would I not want to be in a relationship with you or Gus, for god's sake?"

"Because we were the ones who could teach you the most."

"Jesus Christ. You sound like you wrote this out and

memorized it, Claire. I don't believe you." I got up. I hooked
my foot under the rung of my chair and flipped it on its
back. "I swear you're a goddamn stranger to me now."

"Then nothing has changed."

She said this with an odd smile on her face, the smile
of somebody hiding a trick, I thought. She slowly started
to unbutton BT's sweater and I had the crazy idea she was
going to seduce me. She leaned around and hung the
sweater on the back of her chair. The smile was still there.
"I don't want to walk off with her things," she said, "and
you look like you've had enough of me. If your friend gets
home and I'm here, you won't know how to tell her who
I am."

I just stood there dumbly, watching her pull on her
boots and do up the front of her rainjacket. There were
five complicated little clasps that her fingers knew by heart.
Five little door latches closing her up for the day. That
smile is anger, I told myself. It's her cover-up, and covering
up is her greatest flaw. She has flaws, I told myself. She is
righteous, she is controlled. She is guilty of not loving when
called upon to love. "Everything has changed," I told her.
I pulled her up by the arm. "Listen to me, Claire, everything has changed except one thing." She raised her eyebrows at me. "When I need you to stay with me you have
always and are still running away."

"Is that true?" I felt her arm give. It poured through
my hand. She had moved so close to me I couldn't see her
whole face. She had tilted up my chin and held a finger
under it, and her lips had a pink uncertainty I loved as
she brought her whole head down to kiss me. I don't remember how we'd kissed before. I don't even remember
the first time we kissed. Call this the first time. It was. It
was full of that original giving, mine and hers. There was
so much to her lips, they were soft and wide, and I could
almost taste how red they'd suddenly become. For those
seconds I couldn't locate them on my face. They never left

my mouth but they went everywhere. They went all through my body.

We stopped and she told me, "That kiss is a few years coming."

"Claire," I whispered. "I can feel you between my legs."

"Nice."

"Can you?" I asked her. "Feel me?" With her knuckles she was lightly scrubbing my head.

"Everywhere. All up the front of my rainjacket."

"What did you do when I was gone?"

"About that?" she said. "I learned how to dream about you. I spent every night with you for the first year."

"And then?"

"And then one day I saw a woman in the marketplace, a tall island woman carrying a basket on her head, and I envied her, Franny; I envied her so completely, her great height, her lovely drape, even those fifty pounds of bread-fruit in the basket. The strength of her neck, that she could carry that weight, and how quickly and surely she walked on to her business; and the walking itself was her business. I came every day for a week at that same time just to see her. One day it was breadfruit, another day bananas, an-other day fresh black crabs. The crabs moved around in the basket—I could hear them as she passed. The day of the bananas was marvelous, too, because I smelled them before I saw."

"Claire?"

"She seemed like royalty. She might have been. I'm sure I imagined it but it seemed to me at the time that people stepped aside for her. She walked quickly, with great strides, and it seemed that people felt her coming from behind and cleared a path for her."

"How ridiculous. Did they bow?"

"No, nobody bowed, Franny. And it wasn't the royalty I envied, anyway; it was her steady attention. That look.

That walk. I could tell with her there was no waking up from dreams she never wanted to wake up from. She had one set purpose and she moved ahead to it and she was in it at the same time. It was as if she wore her job."

"But, Claire, her job was simple. She sold breadfruit. Not every job is simple. If I wore my job at the magazine I'd look and feel like a wreck."

"Every job is simple. If you take it on completely, every job fits perfectly. It's exactly where you're meant to be, that step, that weight of fruit or crabs. I stopped dreaming of you, Franny, and started dreaming of that woman. Only she was me."

"And after that you never thought of me again?"

Claire was laughing. "One night, I'll never forget, she came to me in a dream, but instead of a basket on her head she carried a bicycle."

"So you never thought of me?"

"Thought of you?" She looked at me as if she'd just remembered who I was. "Oh my poor sweet. I thought of you often. I was very faithful to you."

"That's funny, Claire. Leading a monk's life it would have been hard not to be."

"I'm not talking about that, Franny. The only way I can be faithful to you or anyone else is to be grateful for our time together. Who cares who I go to bed with?"

"I do!"

"I thought I didn't mean enough to you anymore to argue. How can it matter to you whose body I go to bed with?"

"You *did* have lovers!" I jumped back from her as if she were a sudden heat or chill. "I can see it in you. What is it? Is there a certain kind of lovemaking allowed for celibate people? Was it that man with the shark? Was it a child, Claire? that little boy who wore your shirt? that orphan?"

"Franny."

"I don't mind the thought of you having sex, Claire."

"You hate it," she said.

"I don't mind it." I was shaking my head. "But the goddamn pose of it all, that's what I hate. Showing that pure and virginal face to the world—not just you, all of you there, anyone hiding away in a monastery. When what's really going on in there is exactly what's going on out here, but you're scolding us for it! Our passion! Our—god forbid—lust! People losing themselves to each other: That's a courageous act, Claire! A hell of a lot tougher than losing yourself to God. Try it sometime!"

I shouted the last of this to the floor. I couldn't look at her anymore, she looked so sincerely surprised.

"Franny," she said. I squatted down and hugged my knees and closed my eyes. "Franny." As she bent over, the rainjacket brushed against me like an impersonal skin.

"Take that thing off," I told her. She didn't take it off. "I hate it touching me."

"You're agonizing," she said. "You don't have to agonize. Let me tell you a few things and then I'll never tell you anything else as long as I live."

I looked up at her. "Listen to you."

"Okay. One: It was never a monastery, it was an ashram. We took no vows of celibacy. Celibacy was never assumed. It was a preference for most of us most of the time, that's all. If we'd wanted to screw we would have gone somewhere else, Hawaii or somewhere, Waikiki Beach. Somewhere where the libido level was above subnormal."

"I get it."

"Another thing: I would never scold you for anything, and least of all for your passion. I love your passion, believe me, though I used to confuse it for romance. I want your passion. I want the blows, and I want the peace between blows. I want to feel so much it hurts!"

"Then you still confuse it for romance," I said.

She shook her head. "That edge where you live your life, Franny, I want to be back on it. I've been on it."

"When?"

"I want to be taken apart and have the lovemaking put me together again. I want to be raw and foolish. I want to be imperfect. I know when I'm perfect I'm cheating somebody out of something else. It's not me then. There's no such Claire."

"You're not perfect, Claire."

"I'm not perfect," she repeated. She was crouched over me now. She had her boots on, and her jacket. A couple of bobby pins held the handkerchief in place on her head. She looked like a visitor to the earth. The scar on her cheek was shining. There was a brilliant oddness to her and my good angel wished her everlasting life. This wish loosened my memory, and while we hung there, Claire and I, a particular memory fell out. A light fell across it, a light like white porcelain, like a solid bottle of milk. And though the light was brighter and more significant than the memory, there was no easy way to speak of it, of the light, of how it lifted me in the chest and head and floated my hands. Instead, I talked about what I'd remembered, a thing so meaningless that the difference between what my mind made of it and what the words now made of it came out of me as an accusatory laugh. But I wasn't accusing anyone or anything. I was welcoming home my imagination, the life within my life, whole sight.

"What is it, Franny?"

"I'm remembering that afternoon in your apartment when I wanted to meditate with you."

"You were very earnest. You were funny."

"I was expecting something to happen, but nothing happened, except my legs went to sleep."

Claire had set us up on pillows on the floor in front of the rosewood Buddha. I watched her light incense and a candle. I watched her settle herself, her face, her body and breathing. I watched for some change in her hands because she'd told me she lost feeling in her hands when she meditated. "It's all wrong," she'd laughed. "That's supposed to happen in your head, up between your eyebrows, not in your lap. A sort of emptiness is meant to fill your forehead as you quiet your mind. But what I get is the sensation that everything below the wrist is gone. Now I could understand that, Fran, if I were deaf and using my hands to speak; if my hands were my mouth; if my mouth were my mind."

I expected her hands to glow like an X-ray or disappear altogether as the meditation ran deeper, but nothing happened. She sat straight and motionless with her eyes closed. She didn't seem happier or lighter or better to me. She didn't even seem alive. Fifteen minutes went by. I was sitting cross-legged, as Claire was, and my legs had gone to sleep. Half an hour went by. I dreaded the return of feeling to my feet so I kept them tucked under me. I was disgusted. I was so disappointed. I dragged myself over to the windows in time to see the streetlights come on, one by one, like bubbles stirred up by a slow-moving fish. A dark fish. A street fish. Soon the world would be full of headlights and the little orange lights on top of taxicabs as more fish came to life down there in the narrow passages and gave off light with their breath.

"What's the matter?" Claire had finally come and crouched over me, just as she was now.

"I'm thinking," I told her. I knocked on the window and waved, as if to a friend in the dark.

"Who's out there?"

"I guess I am," I said.

But now we were both out there, looking in through a memory at our old selves, and this softened everything in me. Claire stood up. Her knees creaked. "You're too thin," I told her.

"Invite me to stay for supper then," she laughed.

"Supper." I shook my head. "We're still the only grown women I know who call it supper. Where are you going? Where are you staying? Take the blanket with you, Claire. You'll be warmer."

But she wasn't sleeping on the street, or in the bus station, though I remembered she'd spent nights in parks and cemeteries before to avoid what she called the bad lights of motels. Dragging a boot heel across BT's carpet she drew me a map to the Santa Fe Zen Center. "I'll be there until tomorrow, staying with a friend of mine. He lives in a teepee out behind the main building."

"Oh god," I groaned. "Claire, you're such a relic. Does this gentleman wear a loincloth?"

"No," she laughed, "but he's got a shaved head. He wears a dress, Franny, a skirt, a long black skirt. They all do there."

"Transvestites!"

She nodded. "Spiritual queers."

"Can I come see you?"

"Come after nine, when the evening service is over. Someone in the main building will ask you to take off your shoes."

"Take off my shoes!"

"Yes, Franny. They like to go to bed with footwear."

"Stop, Claire," I held my fingers to her mouth. "You're scaring me."

"I don't mean to scare you," she whispered. She pulled me up against her in a deep hug, released me and was gone.

I stood at the window and watched her, the love of my life, and her sudden ordinariness seemed to fill up the yard. She couldn't get the gate open so she hopped over it and into the street, where at sunset the whole neighborhood was having its moment. Every wall looked like a movie theater marquee, lit up ruby and rose, orange and yellow. And from the street beneath my friend, a long lavender shadow snaked up like smoke, hitting her lower half darkly, so in her boots she seemed to be wading through actual water. "Strong and pure and most unsettling light," I said aloud as the water rose above her head and she was gone. I was on my knees, and that made it a prayer, though I didn't know how to pray or who to pray for.

12

BT insisted I bring her flowers. "You haven't seen her for three years, you may not see her again for three more. Hell, you may never see her again, and you love her, honey, so show her. Bring her flowers."

I tried to explain that Claire and I weren't like that, that we'd never really been romantic together, but BT wouldn't hear it.

"A little courtship won't kill you, Franny. You courted me, remember?"

"BT! Whose side are you on?"

"I'm on my side, sweetheart." She was serious. "You know that. I'm on my side."

A little before nine she pushed me out the door with all her good wishes and half a dozen yellow roses double wrapped in newspaper for the cold walk across town. The rest of that dozen were in her hands. I had turned around in the kitchen and given them to her.

"I'll be at Marion's tonight," she called after me.

"Marion's?"

"Yeah. The house is yours."

Oh women, women, women, I thought. I walked along Canyon Road, where through the lit window of the Dark Star Gallery I could clearly see a boy posing beneath a Nehi sign surrounded by bikes. My show was up and this was one of the early photographs I loved, and to see it now at night, on this night, walking to Claire, calmed and steadied me. I remembered what it had taken to calm and steady that boy; we had changed places for a moment so I stood under the sign and he held the camera. Then he'd taken a picture of his yellow bicycle.

Claire was waiting for me on the porch of the Zen Center. She sat cross-legged on a cushion with a blanket wrapped around her, and she was smoking a cigarette.

"Hello, Franny." She had pulled the blanket up over her head so it hung close about her face, like a veil. There was nothing of her I could see but the hand that held the cigarette, and in the intermittent glow of its ash, her nose and cheeks and a spot of amber in each eye.

From somewhere inside an eerie chanting started up. I thought I saw her body jump, as if an electric current had shot up between her shoulder blades.

"Claire?"

"What is it?" she said.

"Is it all right to touch you here?"

"To touch me?"

"You know. To put my arms around you?"

She looked around, looked at the door at her back. "Of course," she whispered. "And then I want you to take me away from these singing lunatics." She flicked her cigarette into the snow off the porch. "It feels rotten to be smoking again."

I kneeled in front of her and circled her chest and shoulders with one arm. I held the flowers behind my back with the other. But she wasn't all there. Something had come in or gone out of her since the afternoon.

"Where are you, Claire?"

"I'm inside my blanket."

"Where are you?" I said again, not whispering this time and pushing our faces apart so I could look right at her in the dark.

"Okay," she said. "I'm off with my lover in the islands."

"You're what!"

"Shh. The service is going on. They're in the middle of—"

"To hell with them!" I dropped the flowers behind me and grabbed her shoulders and shook her hard. "*You!* Where are *you?*" I pulled the blanket down and with one hand on her chest I pushed her. She went over backwards so her head hit the porch and her legs uncrossed and sprang out from her body. I sat back on my heels and rocked onto the balls of my feet, then back on my heels. I held my head down, staring at the dark porch boards and the darker lines where each board met the next. I counted the lines as far as I could to the left, and to the right, and waited for the next thing to happen.

Claire sat up. "You asked," she said. "If you don't want to know, don't ask." Her voice was shaking. Possibly she was cold.

I didn't look at her. "Go on. Tell me," I said. I heard her light another cigarette. The smoke smelled clean in the cold air and I could smell the tobacco in it.

She didn't say anything for a while, and then she said, "We had a storm out there on the island. This is a way of telling you, Franny. We had a typhoon that knocked the leaves off the trees and left hens in the branches. That was something. All the leaves gone and the trees clucking. I

211

used to stand out in that weather and wait to be moved, picked up and thrown around if that's what it took. Taken somewhere, anywhere. Made to feel. Everyone else got down underground and waited for their shacks to flatten over them. In the ashram, people went to their cells and prayed. Honestly, I don't know what they prayed for. There was no lack of God in weather like that. God blew in on the violence of those storms."

"You're asking people to pray for violence, Claire?"

"I'm not asking people to pray for anything, Franny. I would only ask them to see clearly what they already have. Praying for God doesn't bring God. Praying for a new roof doesn't bring a new roof. You think God makes the hens come home? or do they just come home? And what makes the leaves come back on the trees again? Do they fly up and stick there? I don't think so. All I know is a little while goes by and then a little while longer, and the big broad leaves of the banana, and the fronds of the coconut palm, and the handlike leaves of the breadfruit tree, they're all in their places. I didn't do a thing to help them along and neither did anyone else, and if that's an answered prayer, well that's one way of seeing it. If you quit grabbing for God, there's God. Right where she's always been."

Claire was quiet for a moment. Her cigarette hissed as it hit the snow behind me.

"Miranda and I were lovers. She's the reason I'm home early, the reason I said yes to the farm. She's grabbing so hard for God—they all are there—that she can't even see the God she's got. You know those lakes up high in the mountains, those gorgeous deep lakes that freeze from the bottom up? They're so blue they look black. They look like glass, Franny, like perfect round mirrors framed by the trees. The trees grow up like a wall around them so the wind never touches them. Nothing touches them. Except from the inside, the rise of a fish, but nobody's there to see it. Miranda's a lake like that.

"She was proper. She was a proper Australian doctor and it was two years before we even kissed. She also had wonderful posture, red hair and a tight ass."

"I don't give a damn about her ass, Claire. Shut up about her ass."

"She was utterly selfless, to the point of being bad for herself. All that goodness was ruining her. It might have by now. I got angry at her one night. We had been lovers for a few months and when she gave herself to me in sex I could feel, we could both feel the spirit just shining in her."

"Please, Claire."

"But the rest of the time she was without it. She was all glass surface and faith in something to come. But when it came she wouldn't have it. She wanted to give up the sex because she felt that sexual passion *distracted* a person into one-mindedness, which was her goal as well as mine, I reminded her. *Distracted!* Really! What a woman! 'However you get there, you get there!' I shouted at her. Oh, Franny, I was incensed. I walked on the beach all night and knew the next morning I would leave soon. They could have their cells and solitude. I'd just cured myself of that."

While Claire was talking the chanting had stopped and a light had come on in the window. When I looked at her now she held her hand up to shade her face.

"Claire?"

"What?"

"Why are you here then? With your singing lunatics?"

She shrugged. "Where else would I be?" She pointed at something behind me. "Every time you rock backwards you flatten a little bundle with your boots."

I slid the bundle to Claire and she unwrapped it slowly. "Oh, they were beautiful," she whispered.

"Yeah, but they're ruined."

She nodded. "They have their smell, at least." She crawled over to me and held the back of my head in her hands, and pressed her face hard against mine, her nose against my cheek. "It's not over, is it?" she whispered. "When will it be over? Dear god, let's have it be over."

She released me and went inside and came out again wearing two wool sweaters over her shirt. The handkerchief had come off her head, and she had her white cotton pants tucked into her rubber boots. On the street we walked without talking, Claire a few paces ahead of me, hunched like a pilot over a wheel. She held her roses up in front of her like a torch, their wobbly yellow heads streaming backwards, seeming to flame up her whole body as we moved into the lit circle of one streetlamp after another, out into the open avenues of the town. She was practically running. Her boots clattered around her calves and I had the same sinking feeling I'd had earlier that day about the cold on her neck. I thought she was leading me somewhere until she stopped suddenly, several blocks from the Zen Center, and turned and took both my hands. She nodded back over my shoulder. "There's a loneliness you can practically taste in places like that," she said, "and I think I've outrun it."

We danced in a little bar that night, a bar I knew. We danced slow and close. It was the first time we'd ever danced. Men danced with men and women with women. A blue light darkened Claire's face and darkened her breasts under her light cotton shirt. As we danced we sank deeper and deeper under the dark blue water. We didn't talk much. We touched each other in places made sensual by the simple fact of being in public together, though the bar wasn't crowded and the men and women scattered at little tables watched only each other, as we watched each other. We were the only ones dancing from time to time.

214

"I'd like to get to know that waitress," I said. We were sitting so the sides of our bodies touched. Claire was pinching the back of my neck and tugging my hair. She stopped. "Pull harder," I said.

"We can leave her the flowers."

"Harder. They're your flowers, Claire."

"How did you know to get roses, Franny? I love roses."

"You probably don't remember the time you made soup. You called it Claire's Hundred Vegetable Stew. You'd just read about roughage."

"Was there only one soup? All that winter we lived together? One vegetable soup?"

"There was only one good one. I slept until noon and you woke me up to show me how a cross-sected Brussels sprout looked just like a rose. Your bowl was full of them. You pulled them out of the soup and cut them in half and held them under my nose."

"I remember. And then I climbed into bed with you and we loved all afternoon."

"I don't remember that," I said.

"Oh, yes. That was some of the best love we ever made."

"A little harder, Claire."

"Franny? It's true? You'd really like to get to know that waitress?"

"Not tonight."

"But sometime?"

"Maybe sometime."

She didn't need to be coerced into coming home with me, my friend. She just needed to be led somewhere and that's where I led her.

"Your friend's not home tonight?" she asked. I thought she said it hopefully.

"She's with an old lover."

Claire seemed confused, but said nothing, and I didn't

215

say anything to help her. First, she wanted some tea, and I brought it into the bedroom where she sat, still with all her clothes on, at the foot of the bed.

"Do you do this a lot?" she asked.

"Do what a lot?" I had undressed down to my underwear. I sat and balanced the cup and saucer on my knees and hugged her shoulders.

"Swap houses? Swap lovers? Do you have a lot of lovers, Franny?"

"No."

"Well, is this easy for you? Do you want me here?"

"I want you here. BT wants you here too."

"I don't understand that."

"You did this afternoon. You wanted a house and a barn full of women, remember? You wanted all your lovers and their lovers to come live with you on the farm."

"I didn't want that," she said. "I wanted you, and that may be the only way I can have you."

"You have me now," I whispered to her. "Come on. Lie back. Remember this, Claire? Remember me? *Let me take you to your life.*"

But those words didn't belong to us anymore, we both knew it. She lay back, as if a weariness had forced her there. She sat up again and pulled her sweaters over her head and kicked her boots off. "Your other things?" I said. She shook her head. "Not yet?" She didn't answer. I rubbed her feet. I slid my hands up the legs of her pants and rubbed her calves. I pushed her down gently on the bed and got up to turn the light off. I lowered the window shade against the harsh white of a streetlamp.

"The hour of estrangement," she whispered, and it was there in the room with us, as if the walls held or exhaled it, that indecisive quality of light.

As I loved her, I tried to remember who she was; that she was not this lover or that, but this one, the one I would always love, the only one I would love. I remembered these promises, made by my much younger self, and for the first time now I heard them as Claire must have heard them then, and I blushed with anger and embarrassment. I tried to be rid of them. I had begun to touch her breasts through her shirt and she had said nothing. Now I spread my hands and squeezed her breasts and pulled them toward me. I tried to undo her shirt, then pulled it off her so its buttons caught in her hair. Still she said nothing. I pushed her arms above her head and bit the soft flesh of her upper arms, her armpits, her neck. I sucked each nipple hard so she turned away from me, turned on her side, then on her stomach. I reached under her and found the top of her pants and yanked the elastic down over her hips and ass. She wasn't wearing underwear. She said something I didn't hear. She was pale and thin and hard, her flesh like a smooth bone. I pulled her pants off her, one leg then the next, moving too fast. "Go slow, Franny." She rolled on her side and brought her knees up to her face, almost covering her face. "You don't have any underwear on," I said. "Oh god, Claire, there's the beautiful crack of your ass."

I pulled her feet to me, forcing her legs straight, and I pushed myself roughly between her thighs. I opened my mouth to her cunt so quickly, long before she was ready to let me in. She tried to push me away from her with her palms flat against the tops of my shoulders. She brought her knee up to my face, trying to push me away. "Don't do it, Franny," she said, a hoarse whisper. "I don't want it, don't do it," she said again, but this only made me want her harder.

I struggled to stay with her, and with both legs now and both hands she pushed me off. "Let me!" I hissed at her. Her smell made me crazy and I loved her struggling. I clamped her knees to my ears and knew I could force her to feel me all over her body. "Want me, Claire. You want me." I was digging my fingers into her thighs and she cried out. "Give it to me, *give* it to me," I said. I could have broken both her legs. I had the power. I dug deeper.

We wrestled on the bed and the dark made us no different than lovers. Or she could have been anyone, just a gray shape I reached for over and over again, a body of limbs indistinguishable from my own except the pain they felt, I inflicted. Everywhere I touched her I wanted to hurt her, and once when I was on top of her I bent her arm up over her head until I felt whatever was vital in it snap. She was panting and sobbing, only defending herself at first as if it might pass, all my physical effort might pass right through her if she made herself quiet and calm. But I brought her up to me. I made her see that what was in me was real. I had her by the neck and I brought her face up close to mine in front of the white window shade.

We rolled over and over on the bed, onto the floor. We pulled at each other's hair, and grunted and coiled around each other. She could cover me with her body but I was quicker and stronger than she was. I held her down on the rug. A slow ache came into my right elbow where I'd broken it, and I hated her for the ache and swung at her with my left fist. I swung hard at where I thought her face was. What I hit, gave, and when it gave, everything in me was finished.

Claire didn't move. After some time I got up and turned on the light. I was afraid to look at her so I looked down at my own body first. My thighs were streaked with blood. That blood was on my hands, my arms, drying with the sweat on my belly. There was no part of me that was hurt or bleeding. My skin seemed too pale to be anyone's. I looked at Claire who was balled up on the floor at the foot of the bed, the fingers of one hand spread out across her hair. She was turned away from me. Her right shoulder looked huge. There was blood on the backs of her thighs where I'd dug into her.

Her eye was bleeding and swollen shut. She let me

lift her onto the bed but the one good eye would have nothing to do with me. It ran wildly around the walls and ceiling. That was her out there. We both knew it. She brought her hand up to the eye and pinched the lid down.

"I think my shoulder's broken. It hurts like hell," she said.

I brought her a damp towel for the eye, and covered her and felt how her shoulder was stretched or possibly sprained, but not broken. I switched off the light and lay down with her. I could feel her good eye open to the dark and her mouth open to say something, but she never said it. I could feel what old, old friends we must be to lie this way, like old people with our pains and regrets, each in the dark fingering her hurts, worrying, waiting to be forgiven, not by the other but by our own selves. We slept, and in the early morning when I reached out to hold her I was still asleep, and slept on until noon, alone in the bed and not knowing it, clutching only the pillow to me.

13

She had gone home. She dragged her trunk to the bus station and got on the early Greyhound to Chicago. No one helped her. No one had been awake to help her. I pictured her carting the trunk on her back like an Asian porter through the dawn, but then I remembered her shoulder and the knot came into my stomach for the hundredth time that day.

At the Zen Center her friend, Joseph, gave me the news of her and a small package wrapped neatly in a brown paper bag. Inside was the towel I'd used to cover her eye. She'd washed all the blood out of it and dried it, or someone had. No note. No nothing. I walked to a small park and sat on the cold metal seat of a swing, and pressed my face to that towel as I'd done how many years before in Claire's little apartment, to have her with me when she wouldn't be. And I cried at what had been the sweetness of my sleep, knowing she was sleeping next to me; knowing

220

her soul healed mine while our minds went away at night, no matter how broken we were. But she hadn't been there, and I'd slept as if she had. When I picked her up off the floor and laid her on the bed it was close to two, and the first bus left at four. She could only have waited as long as it took for my breathing to settle, then she'd dressed. I imagined her hugging her right arm close against her body to keep from feeling its pain, and I thought of her two sweaters. How had she fit herself into them? Had she worn them at all or only draped them around her, hanging one in front, the other in back like a sandwich board? Had she looked at me? I wondered. Of course she'd looked at me. Had she leaned over the bed to look at me? Had she touched me? Had she cried over me? Had Claire ever cried over me? Had both eyes cried?

"Let go of it," said BT. "You take a thing to its end, there's enough courage in that. Don't kick yourself. Don't kick anybody. If it ends badly, or not the way you wanted, well so let it be. I'm sure your friend Claire knows all this. What do you think that farm's for, Franny? It's to take up her days."

And I saw that, too, Claire getting old among the chickens, or warming her hands by a flaming barrel of trash, watching its smoke slip down her solitary hill and fill up the valley; and nothing was sadder to me from time to time. I remembered something she'd said the night we danced. "Truth is wisdom," she told me. "Truth is compassion. Wisdom I can learn from the chickens; compassion I need people for."

"Well, my friend, there goes your precious solitude," I said to her.

She laughed close to my ear. "And I'll be the happiest woman in the world to see it go."

In the spring I had a letter from her, damning April and every stubborn tree, as if the whole season were a reminder that her will was not enough to make things flower and leaf out. What was withheld she took so to heart, Claire did, and now I understood that she always had, and that her own withholding had been the hardest for her, even harder and more disappointing for her than for me.

> And I don't hope much. I don't know about us. I know you're sitting in the seat next to the me of me, and when the lights dim we hold hands. I know I am much stronger. My shoulder and eye forgive you. And forgive me, but I use both now as if they were only my body parts and not the last two places you touched me deeply. I feel, and when I feel I still want you. This doesn't matter. Where there is love, we can ruin love. Even the sex couldn't save us. But the times we've been only us, engaged in each other, not calling it afterward love or hate, those matter. You have been with me all morning and are still, bright sun on the last, maddening snow. I don't care what happens to us as long as some of the moments on the way to what happens are as deep and full as this one.
>
> Om Shanti,
> Claire

They didn't call for an answer, those words, but those strange syllables—*Om Shanti, Claire*—whatever they meant, they sang their way into me, into the next year of my life. I was twenty-six, and hungrier than I'd ever been, an actual, physical hunger. I grew an inch. I ate white rice and bean curd, and grew another inch. I moved out of BT's house and loved her better that way, and learned to make love to other women from a large place in me instead of in order to win them. I learned to make love to them the way Claire had always made love to me. *Om Shanti, Claire,* I thought to myself every time circumstance beguiled me into another unfamiliar bed.

No summer rains, no snow. On my twenty-seventh

birthday a dust storm beat at the windows until two of them gave way. Another letter came from Claire. She had ducks and chickens and goats, she wrote; she had a horse, a lover. A lover, Claire! I held the pages to me for a moment, unable to keep reading while my demon flared and finally left me. It's no use, friend, I laughed. I will always feel it, feel you, feel all the heat of our old connection no matter how or where you try and hide your newest love, this one crouched between goat and horse in the barn.

But it was clear, as I read on, that rather than hiding this woman from me, Claire was only giving me the truest sense of the calm and ordinary way she wanted to have everything now, including a lover, in her life.

I thought for the longest time it would take the big pleasures, or one big pleasure to cure me. I don't know, like playing the piano really beautifully or saving a friend from death. But here at Platypus Farms (you see I've named the place after your idea of me) I'm a better plumber than pianist. I see it's the little pleasures that bring me back to myself. I still desire things, everything sometimes. And just then the iris blooms at the pump house, or the ice falls. I still make distinctions, between ice and iris, her and her, me and all the rest. But then she or all the rest arrive with a home-cured ham, and dust the snow off my swing and sit in it, or sit inside on my four little broken-backed chairs, giving me so precisely what I need, and all cocking the same head at once to the yip of a fox out hunting in this fickle weather, that the distinctions are laughable. I'm laughable. We're laughable. Even though we aren't exactly that either.

My dream is to set up a lot of fourposter beds between the rows in the greenhouse, and someday look in on all my friends and lovers just getting up. Some of them are standing ankle-deep in spinach, tomatoes to the waist. Some of them are still making love. Some of them are sleeping—a bent knee tenting the sheet is all I recognize of them anymore. She used to lie that way, I remember. We used to love that way. Those are her breasts floating in green above the little yellow tomato flowers. They all used to be you, Franny dear, though now only one of them is you. The one in the middle whose face, from behind a fan of spinach, is looking out through my eyes, remembering too.

What I remembered as I lay her letter down, was Claire's longing for passion, for *my* passion as she once said, and how I'd always felt the burden of that longing because it was the only thing I ever knew she was asking me for, and I couldn't—who could?—give it to her. She had it herself. She had always had it herself. But what she saw in me and thought it was, it often wasn't.

Now something had led her to it; she had been brought back to herself, and I was never so drawn to her. I told her nothing of this but held it in my heart so it became the real ground for all I said or did. It always had been, Claire had been. I knew this. I had no idea if I'd ever see her again, or be with her. I only knew she made it easy for me now to love every woman I loved, and before she had made it impossible.

Soon enough, I did see her again, and then as often as I looked for her I saw her. The first time was shortly after her letter arrived, on a drive through northern New Mexico. I was alone and driving, as I often did, for the pleasure of driving. It was evening and the motion of the car gave the hills a blurred look, as if they were something from memory and not in this world at all. There wasn't a single tree along my road, nothing linear and close to cast a shadow. After several miles of this I stopped and rested my head on the steering wheel, and when I looked up again, there was Claire.

She was a tall woman walking a few yards ahead of me, away from me in the road, and balanced upside down on her head was a bicycle. She wore the seat low on her forehead, and her left arm reached forward to hold the handlebars. Her right one swung free and her hand was cupped, like a swimmer pulling through water.

I honked my horn—it was an idiotic instinct, but I was parked in the grass and loose gravel and couldn't make myself step out onto the pavement that might have connected me to her. The intricate part of her shadow, the wheels and spokes of the bicycle, slid off the hood of my car as I watched. The sun was low in front of us, off her left shoulder. It was a blinding sun, and as she walked she became part of what blinded me. Only her shadow showed me that she moved forward, whoever she was. It skittered along the shoulder of the road where a bicycle belonged, and I thought I might see a stone roll over or a loop of dust fly up, or hear the popping sound of a tire—it was real enough to me, that shadow, though the actual woman I was willing to doubt.

I started the car, then turned it off again. I stopped looking ahead of me and for a long time let my head move from side to side. I remembered that this was the hour of estrangement, the hour we'd loved, Claire and I, and it was bound to bring us anything, everything. I turned on my lights and drove along the side of the road until I was certain the dusk light hid nothing from me, that I had only seen a ghost and imagined a tall shadow, then I swung back onto the pavement in the direction of home.